the Near and the Far

David Carlin is an award-winning writer and creative artist. His books include *The Abyssinian Contortionist*, *Our Father Who Wasn't There*, and *Performing Digital*. David wrote and co-produced the radiophonic feature *Making Up*, which won four Gold and Silver awards at the 2016 New York Festivals International Radio Awards. David is vice-president of the international NonfictioNOW Conference, and Associate Professor of Creative Writing, co-founder of the non/fictionLab research group, and co-director of the WrICE program at RMIT University.

Francesca Rendle-Short is an award-winning novelist, memoirist, and essayist. She is the author of *Imago* and the acclaimed novel-cum-memoir *Bite Your Tongue*. Her work has appeared in a wide range of Australian and international publications, including *Best Australian Science Writing*, *Overland*, and *The Essay Review*, and her artwork is in the collection of the State Library of Queensland. Francesca is Associate Professor of Creative Writing at RMIT University, where she is co-founder and co-director of the non/fictionLab research group and the WrICE program.

the Near and the Far

new stories from the Asia-Pacific region

DAVID CARLIN and FRANCESCA RENDLE-SHORT

SCRIBE
Melbourne • London

Scribe Publications
18–20 Edward St, Brunswick, Victoria 3056, Australia
2 John St, Clerkenwell, London, WC1N 2ES, United Kingdom

First published by Scribe 2016

Typeset in Adobe Caslon Pro 11 / 17 by the publishers
Printed and bound in Australia by OPUS Group

A CiP record for this title is available from the National Library of Australia.

9781925321562 (paperback)
9781925307795 (e-book)

 The WrICE program (2014–2017) has been generously
supported by the Copyright Agency Cultural Fund.

 NONfictionLAB

scribepublications.com.au
scribepublications.co.uk

CONTENTS

THE NEAR AND THE FAR

FOREWORD

Alice Pung

'Wherever you go, go with all your heart.' — *Confucius*

I didn't do much travelling until I was twenty-seven. A strict Chinese upbringing coupled with the anxieties of genocide-surviving parents meant that I went through my university days living vicariously through the travel tales of my worldlier friends. The first time I went overseas by myself, I expected everything to be different: of course the architecture and food, but also the very material of the buildings, the composition of the leaves on the trees. I expected to see a substantially different world and was disappointed that the city of Beijing — apart from some historical quarters — looked like *a city*. I tried very hard to look for difference, so I could write original stories to send back home to my editor. I did not understand then that to write about a place is not to simply pick out points of difference, but to search for the things that make us commonly human, that this was the difference between an anecdote and a story with a heartbeat.

The Near and The Far is one of those rare travel anthologies, combining fiction with poetry and longform essays, each piece revealing a real insider's experience of inhabiting a different world without exoticising the foreign. Each story has a centre — whether philosophical, moral, or political — and yet none of them are didactic.

Omar Musa's tale of revelatory *dis*orientation and Maxine Beneba Clarke's exploration of ignorance and fear are rooted in a warmth for characters usually portrayed as pitiable or loathsome. Cate Kennedy watches with her poet's eye but does not presume to know those who populate the other side of the Vietnam War, while Harriet McKnight's politically charged vignettes are skilfully nuanced.

Stories about place often evoke memories of family, such as Jennifer Down's beautiful story of kids bonded by adversity, Joe Rubbo's brilliant tale of absent fathers that centres on the arrival of a trampoline, and Robin Hemley's poignant father–daughter narrative that captures the teenage voice perfectly. In these stories, culture is not *done*, it is lived.

Suchen Christine Lim's story explores a silent and stoic love that allows her to understand the meaning of family, while Alvin Pang examines through ethereal mythology the origins of identity and belonging. Melissa Lucashenko's stellar, heartbreaking piece is about the laconic friendship of two women bonded by a mutual loss so immense it overtakes the landscape of the story, while Francesca Rendle-Short's '1:25,000' encompasses decades of love and longing through the chasm of the Grand Canyon. And indeed, the person or place at the centre of the journey, once a stranger, becomes a cherished lover, as in Jhoanna Lynn B. Cruz's exquisitely tender 'Comadrona', or in Nguyen Bao Chan's achingly nostalgic poems.

All art and travel is about risk-taking. Great literary risks are clearly evinced in Melody Paloma's poem filled with the debris of daily life and pop culture, Amarlie Foster's exploration of anxiety and art through palm readings, Nyein Way's metaphysical, playful, cerebral 'Joycean realities on paper', and Xu Xi's humorous insight into 'The Significant Years' before Google: all original and playful answers to the question of journeying. However, risk-taking appears as the central theme of Laura Stortenbeker's light-and-dark coming-of-age 'Floodlit', and Bernice Chauly's impassioned, frenetic piece about Malaysia's Reformasi.

Finally, David Carlin cheekily acknowledges the faceless people who can often be appropriated for their culture in literature (including a Thai Elvis impersonator!), as does Laurel Fantauzzo's funny 'instructional' piece about the inherent unknowability of a culture: 'no one is a mere instrument of your movement'.

This is why I took the risk of resorting to cliché by beginning with a Confucius quote. The first quote I heard attributed to the Chinese scholar was in primary school, when a gappy-toothed boy told me — with fake Oriental accent — 'Confucius say man who go through airport turnstile too quick arrive to Bang Kok.' But when, as an adult, I visited Qufu, Confucius' birthplace, and saw the immense reverence the villagers — literate or not — had for the man, I simultaneously understood both the tacit history of ignorant racism back home and the eye-opening wonders and possibilities of travel. The stories in this anthology perform just this function, by opening the heart to both empathy and awe.

INTRODUCTION

David Carlin and Francesca Rendle-Short

For centuries Macassan traders zigzagged across the waters between the Indonesian islands and Australia, fishing for *trepang*, or sea cucumber, and exchanging goods and culture with Australia's Aboriginal nations — songs and stories, art and language. Among all the thousands of communities in South-East Asia and Australia, there has been a constant to and fro of people, animals, plants, and objects, exotic, precious, and mundane. Borders have been made and remade, foreign armies suffered and driven out. In this most hybridised of regions, everything is interlaced, whether on the surface or below. We share the same winds and the same ocean currents.

And yet, sometimes it feels like we hardly know one another, or where one another comes from. We feel like strangers. We go on cheap holidays to each other's countries but never really meet: we don't sit down together at a table, with a barbeque or lazy Susan.

Our different colonial experiences have left long shadows across our imaginations. Too often those of us who are settlers don't recognise those whose land we've taken, or even that we've taken it. It was said we lived in 'outposts' — the 'Far East', they called it, with Australia farther still, almost lost, down in the Southern Ocean. It's not surprising that we still look to Europe and America for our cultural headline acts: David Bowie could only come from Brixton, not from Bali. The far feels near, and the near feels far away.

So imagine a group of writers — from Brisbane and Kuala Lumpur, from Singapore, Yangon, Queanbeyan, and beyond — gathered together around a large dining table under a swishing ceiling fan in an old Penang apothecary. Or in a room above a river strung with yellow fishnets in Vietnam. One by one these writers take it in turns to share their writing, stories, and art. They don't know each other. Everyone is awkward and embarrassed. They are offering the gift of their culture in its rawest, roughest form. The work is fresh and unfinished. It might have been written just that morning.

Imagine food from the local region on the table as sustenance and comfort: samosas and Xiang Si prunes, watermelon, rambutan, and mangosteen. After the first person reads aloud there is a long silence, impossible to interpret. The tall poet from Singapore leans in and says, gravely: *what do we do now?*

Into this void, the conversation starts to flow, slow and stuttering at first, riotous before long. Each person takes the risk in turn. Some of the writers are older, wise grandees, but still confess to being often lost. Others are young and wide-eyed, but with quiet, crystal voices.

Every writer wants a reader, because no writer can hear her own work from the other side. Every writer wonders: how does it strike *you*, dear reader? Does it move you? Does it immerse you in its rhythms? Does it make you care? Around the table in Penang or Hoi An, each writer wants to know: you, who come from somewhere very different to me, maybe with another language, with different gods and different lullabies — how do you hear this story, this essay, or this poem? Does it sing to you? Does it jar, perhaps, here, or here?

Where can the lines of our writing lead us?

The Near and The Far is an invitation to pull up a chair and join the table, listening in, as it were, to the conversation made by these stories, essays, and poems. The hope is that you too can become part of this growing conversation between the cultures of our region, whether it's in your imagination or over the metaphorical back fence with your neighbours. Bring your own treats, be they lamingtons or laksa.

The table itself is courtesy of a project called WrICE (Writers Immersion and Cultural Exchange), started in 2014 by a group of us in the non/fictionLab at RMIT University in Melbourne. WrICE is a program of reciprocal residencies and cultural events focused on writers and writing from Australia and the Asia-Pacific. With support from the Copyright Agency Cultural Fund, WrICE, in its first two years, invited the extraordinary group of writers whose work is now collected in this book. Residencies took place in George Town, Penang, Hoi An, Vietnam, and in the Yarra Valley in Australia, with workshops, readings, and performances in Singapore, Castlemaine, Hanoi, Melbourne, and Footscray.

The mornings of a WrICE residency are spent writing and thinking, each of the writers moving quietly around their hotel or guesthouse, immersed in their own thoughts and imaginative worlds. Each writer finds their own creative space, making work as they see fit. When lunchtime comes, some venture out, in groups, to find food. They take in the local sounds and smells, and soak up the patterns and delicacies of their temporary home, whether it be Little India in Penang, the fish market in Hoi An, or among the world's tallest hardwoods in the Yarra Ranges. Other writers prefer to be alone: to whistle off along the river past the square yellow fishnets on a bicycle or to keep writing in the cool of the bistro, headphones on, an iced ginger drink to hand.

In the afternoons, the writers gather around the table.

Trust and friendship grow out of the vulnerability and risk inherent in the act of sharing writing-in-progress. The cultural exchange is premised on a spirit of mutual respect and open-hearted generosity. After the residency, it flows on into public events: readings, workshops, and discussions. The shared cultural and artistic experience generates threads of connection that endure across distance and time, resulting in collaborations and dialogues, including this collection.

The Near and The Far. Think of it as dispatches from our neighbourhood, brief melodies from the local air. One or two might feel as familiar as your own skin. (It all depends on where you start from.) Others might take you a long way out from any shore you recognise, and yet when you wash up in some other place, perhaps in the end, that too might feel a little closer.

THE
NEAR

DREAMERS

Melissa Lucashenko

'Gimme an axe.'

The woman blurted this order across the formica counter. When the shopkeeper turned and saw her brimming eyes he took a hasty step backwards. His rancid half-smile, insincere to begin with, vanished into the gloomy corners of the store. It was still very early. Outside, tucked beneath a ragged hibiscus bush, a hen cawed a single, doubtful note. Inside was nothing but this black girl and her highly irregular demand.

The woman's voice rose an octave.

'Give us a Kelly, Mister, quick. I got the fiver.'

She rubbed a grubby brown forearm across her wet eyes. Dollars right there in her hand, and still the man stood, steepling his fingers in front of his chest.

It was 1969. Two years earlier there had been a referendum. Vote Yes for Aborigines. Now nobody could stop blacks going where they liked. But this just waltzing in like she owned the place, mind you. No *please*, no *could* I. And an axe was a man's business. Nothing good could come of any Abo girl holding an axe.

The woman ignored the wetness rolling down her cheeks. She laid her notes on the counter, smoothed them out. Nothing wrong with them dollars. Nothin' at all. She pressed her palms hard onto the bench.

'Are. You. Deaf?'

'Ah. Thing is. Can't put my hand to one just at the ah. But why not ah come back later ah. Once you've had a chance to ah.'

The woman snorted. She had had fifty-one years of coming back later. She pointed through an open doorway to the dozen shining axes tilted against the back wall. On its way to illuminate these gleaming weapons, her index finger silently cursed the man, his formica counter, his cawing hen, his come back later, his ah, his doorway, and every Dugai who had ever stood where she stood, ignorant of the jostling bones beneath their feet.

Her infuriated hiss sent him reeling.

'Sell me one of them good Kellys, or truesgod Mister I dunno what I'll do.'

As twenty-year-old Jean got off the bus, she rehearsed her lines.

'I'm strong as strong. Do a man's eight hours in the paddock if need be. Giss a chance, missus.'

When Jean reached the dusty front yard of the farm on Crabbes Creek Road and saw the swell of May's stomach, hard and round as a melon beneath her faded cotton dress, she knew that she couldn't work here. When May straightened, smiling, from the wash basket, though, and mumbled through the wooden pegs held in her teeth Jean? Oh thank God you're here, she thought that perhaps she could.

Ted inched up the driveway that afternoon in a heaving Holden sedan. Shy and gaunt, he was as reluctant to meet Jean's eye as she was to meet his. This white man would not be turning her door handle at midnight. She decided to stay for a bit. If the baby came out a girl she would just keep going, and anyway, maybe it would be a boy.

The wireless in the kitchen said the Japanese were on the back foot in New Guinea but from Crabbes Creek the war seemed unlikely and very far away. What was real was endless green paddocks stretching to where the scrub began, and after that the ridge of the Border Range, soaring to cleave the Western sky. The hundred-year-old ghost gums along the creek, the lowing of the cows at dawn: these things were real. A tame grey lizard came to breakfast on the verandah, and occasionally Jean would glimpse the wedgetails wheeling far above the mountain, tiny smudges halfway to the sun. May had seen both eagles on the road once, after a loose heifer had got itself killed by the milk truck. You couldn't fathom the hugeness of them, and the magnificent curve of their talons, lancing into the unfortunate Hereford's flank.

Jean fell into a routine of cleaning, cooking, helping May in the garden, and sitting by the wireless at night until Ted began to snore or May said ah well. Of a morning, as she stoked the fire and then went out with an icy steel bucket to milk the bellowing Queenie, Jean would hear May retching and spewing in the thunderbox. One day, two months after she first arrived, there was blood on the marital sheets. Jean stripped the bed and ordered May to lie back down on clean linen. Then she took Ted's gun off the wall and shot a young roo from the mob which considered the golden creek flats their own particular kingdom. A life to save another life. Jean made broth from the roo tail. And you can just lie there 'til it's your time, she said crisply. It's not like I can't manage that little patch of weedy nothing you like to call a garden.

The life inside May fought hard to hang on. Her vomiting eased, and as the weeks passed the terror slowly left her face. When her time drew very near, an obvious question occurred to May. Didn't Jean want children of her own? A husband?

Not really, said Jean, and who would I marry anyway, and is that Ted home already.

May ignored the possibility of Ted. The war will be over soon, there'll be lots of blokes running about the place. You said you like babies.

Yes, Jean said, expressionless. Other people's babies. Now lie flat, or I'll never hear the end of it from Himself.

You mean from you, laughed May, for the doctor had said the danger was past. Baby kicked happily now whenever it heard Ted's voice coming up the stairs.

The next week, Ted drove his wife into Murwillumbah at speed, churning dust and scaring fowl all the way to the hospital. They returned three days later with a squalling bundle on the back seat. Jean held her breath, waiting to discover if she could stay.

We called him Eric, Ted told the water tank proudly. After me old dad.

Eric, repeated Jean, reaching down to stroke a tiny pink cheek.

Later May reported the doctor's verdict: make the most of this one, because there would be no more babies for her.

Eric was a plump, laughing baby, and then an adored toddler, always wandering, always in the pots and pans.

Come to Jean-Jean, she would cry, and Eric would ball his little fists and hurtle joyfully into her, clutching at her shins. She lifted him high in the air, both of them squealing with delight, until May came out laughing too, and demanded her turn. If the child cried in the night, it didn't matter to him who arrived to comfort him. Eric was at home in the world, because the world had shown him only love and tenderness.

'If it wasn't for the fact that I feed him,' May said casually, tucking herself back into her blouse one day, 'I don't think he'd know that I'm his mother, and not you.'

'Oh, he does!' protested Jean, feeling a sudden thread of fear unspooling in her gut. 'And he's the spit of you, anyway. What would he want with a mother like me?'

May glanced at Jean's brown face, her black eyes and matchstick limbs.

'You're not all that dark. You're more like Gina Lollobrigida,' she said generously. 'Exotic. Plenty of men would want you for a wife.'

'But would I want them?' Jean retorted, a question that had never occurred to May.

After that, Jean held the boy a little less when his mother was around. She let May go to him at night, and was careful to be outside more often helping Ted in the paddock when Eric needed his afternoon bath. May thought they were pals, but Jean knew she could be flung away from the farm with one brief word, catapulted back to the Mission even, if she couldn't scrape a better life up out of her own effort and wits.

May confessed tearfully one day that she had briefly allowed Eric — now struggling on her lap to regain his lost freedom — to stray into the Big Paddock. 'I actually felt my heart stop. I never knew you could love anyone so much.'

But I did, thought Jean, with a pang so fierce it made her gasp.

'He's a terror for wandering, all right. Pity we can't bell him like Queenie,' was what she finally managed.

May caught the bus to town and returned with a tinkling ribbon which had had six tiny silver bells sewn onto it by kind Mrs O'Connell. With the ribbon pinned between his shoulder blades, Eric could be heard all over the house and yard, a blue cattle bitch lurking by his side as constant as a shadow.

The second time Eric got himself lost, he was gone half an hour. They finally found him playing in the mud on the far side of the duck house, three strides from the dam, the ribbon torn off by the wire around the vegie patch. The women, who had each thought that the other was watching Eric, quietly resolved to say nothing to Ted. That night Jean woke the household screaming that a black snake had got in and bitten the baby — but it was only a bad dream.

It was the barking that alerted them to Eric's third disappearance, a few weeks later. Peeling spuds on the verandah, Jean became aware of the dog's frenzied yelps, and realised that she hadn't heard Eric's bell for a minute or more. She rocketed to her feet, sending spuds all over the silky-oak floorboards, and ran blindly to the yard where the dog was circling in agitation.

Jean and May circumnavigated the house, then the paddocks, with no result. Eric would not be found. A search party fanned out, desperate for clues. Here the boy had scratched at the damp creek bank with a twig from the largest gum. Here he had uprooted one of Queenie's dry pats, to discover what crawling treasures lay beneath. But the signs petered out where the pasture of the Big Paddock turned into scrubby foothills, and nothing was revealed — not that day, nor the next, nor in the awful weeks that followed — that could bring Eric back to them. The boy had quite simply vanished.

Nobody could fathom why Ted and May kept the dark girl on. But who else would understand why Ted could never go straight to the Big Paddock in the mornings anymore, and took the long way past the dam instead? Who else shared May's memory of Eric tilting his head to eat his porridge? The high tinkling bell-note of a king parrot's call made Jean catch May's eye, and neither of them had to say a word. And so the terrible thing which would have driven any other three people far apart instead bound them together.

In spring, Ted planted a silky oak sapling between the house and the gate. At its foot lay an engraved granite boulder. May took to sitting beside Eric's rock at odd hours of the day and night, gazing past the ghost gums, searching the distant hills.

When the wet season arrived they sat, waiting to see what would wash down to them from the forested gullies. But the foaming brown floodwaters of the creek revealed as little as the search parties. Their vigil, like all of Ted's endless Sunday tramping, scouring the hills, was in vain.

Queenie still lowed at dawn, demanding to be milked. The eagles still wheeled over the ridge. The tame grey lizard still came for crumbs in the morning. Jean ventured out from the house more than before; she learned from Ted how to rope and brand calves, and then to jerkily drive the cattle truck into town. Good as any man with stock, he told her boots. Nobody blamed her; nobody asked her to leave.

Perhaps, Jean reflected wryly, after three more summers had passed, perhaps May *was* a friend, after all.

It was two decades, and a new war in Korea come and gone, before the government letter arrived. *It has been determined by our engineering division.* Ted looked up from the Big Paddock at the hills to be sliced in half by the new highway. May began slamming doors. Soon bulldozers arrived, and men with dynamite. Ted scratched at his scalp. The jungled ridge belonged to the memory of Eric, not to the government.

But then what if they turned something up. Hard to know what to think, really.

When the first young protestors came to the door, Ted walked away, but May dried her hands on a tea towel and listened. Don't bother the stock, she told them, and shut them bloody gates. A village of yurts and Kombis sprang up near the creek.

Jean and Ted shook their heads. Girls in muslin dresses staggered up to the house, sunburnt, dehydrated, bitten by spiders. The trees are our brothers, Jean was informed by a boy who needed a lift to hospital the next day, concussed by a falling limb. A jolly fellow with an earring fell into the campfire and burned half his face off. At month's end, the remnant kernel of protesters tried, and failed, to scale the largest of the gum trees to stage a sit-in in its canopy.

It wasn't ultimately clear to the district who should bear the blame for the inferno. Most said the protestors, obviously, for lighting campfires in the first place, or May for allowing the city-bred fools on the place. Some blamed the cop who had deliberately kicked coals towards nylon tents, determined that the hippies be driven out. A few even blamed Ted for failing to maintain his rutted driveway better, so that the fire truck couldn't get to the paddock in time.

After the sirens had faded, and the night was at an end — the firefighters had picked up all their tools and taken them home, and the Kombis had pulled away from the charred ground in disgrace — Ted, May, and Jean slumped on the verandah, filthy and almost too tired for sleep. A profound silence fell upon the farm. No stock remained alive to bellow. The only sound was the faint shushing of a light breeze through the few pathetic trunks still standing in the blackened smear that had been the Big Paddock. That, and a strange high tinkling from beyond the creek.

Bone-weary, Jean and May stared at each other. Then they ran, flinging great black clouds of ash in their wake. They forded the creek and ploughed their way through the fire-thinned scrub, until at last they stood below an enormous tallowwood, halfway up the mountain. It was a tree Ted knew; he had eaten a sandwich beneath it more than once on his Sunday treks. The fire had reached it, licked its trunk, caused it to shudder and tremble, but not to fall.

'There.'

Jean pointed up. Ted and May craned their necks, squinting in the first faint streak of dawn light. What tinkled above them was a narrow thread, dislodged from its resting place by the force of the fire, and spinning now in the breeze which blew across the empty paddock. The merest ghost of a belled ribbon, it had been wedged tight in the eagle's nest for thirty years.

Get me an axe, thought Jean.

ML: This story was born from experiences in the Scenic Rim of South-East Queensland and grew to fruition in the very different setting of Penang, where I was lucky enough to be on a WrICE residency in 2015.

Surrounded by the sights and smells of Chinese-Malay George Town, good-luck firecrackers making a noisy soundscape to work within, I drew upon a local Queensland incident where a young woman disappeared, presumed murdered, in the high peaks of the Border Ranges. Her body has never been found; when I lived in the Scenic Rim, we always used to wonder what the summer floods might bring down off the mountains. I ended up setting the story in a slightly different region, on the New South Wales side of those mountains, in homage to Crabbes Creek, an area I love and have spent some time in over the years. I incorporated the image of a wandering boy wearing a bell — in reality, something that was pinned to my brother as a child, him being a great wanderer. This story shows what can come out when there are absolutely no parameters to work within — no theme was set, no length prescribed. I just had to produce something to share with a mob of mostly unknown (to me) Asian and Australian writers. I didn't know this story was waiting within me until I sat down in George Town. And that's always the best way to find something truly original.

FLOODLIT

Laura Stortenbeker

Ella is sitting on the edge of the sink in just a crop top and jeans. Her chest is flat like a new road. She's not shy to be undressed with these girls. She's doing a stuttering dance with her arms, head tilted back, touching the mirror. Under the white lights of the bathroom the three of them look younger than they are, even with everything they're doing to look older. Their ritual is to get ready at K's. Her dad works a lot. They're listening to Top 40 radio hits and every now and then one of them turns the dial on the speakers and the whole room throbs.

K has the thinnest eyebrows. She tweezes at them fast and mean. Her eyelids are a blue-blood colour, her voice wavers when she sings. The air in the room is stale because Yasmin is smoking a cigarette; Marlboro Reds, whatever was in her mum's purse that morning. The girls were quietly drunk at first but it hasn't taken long for it to catch up with them. This isn't their first time.

Ella's arms tremble when she reaches to the back of her hair; it has to be right, so she fixes her braids for the third time tonight. Now, Yasmin is putting on extra make-up to cover her bad skin and the yellowed bruise on the side of her cheek. She applies less pressure to the discoloured area even though it stopped hurting a week before.

'Who did that to you?' says K.

'My sister,' says Yasmin.

'No, really.'

'Yeah, my sister.' Then she drops her shoulders and shakes her head and says *family* but she spells it out, f-a-m-i-l-y, like it's a word she's afraid to say.

'That's kind of fucked up,' says Ella. 'My brother hits me pretty bad but not on my face.'

'I have something for you guys,' says K and Yasmin looks relieved that their eyes are off her. K's smirking in a proud, defiant way. She holds out two clenched fists, asking them to choose one. Yasmin slaps at K's right hand and K jerks away.

'Fuck, you'll make me drop them.' She flips her fist over and opens her palm.

'What are those?' says Ella.

'Don't be dumb, bitch, they're pills.'

Yasmin rubs at her throat. Her necklace catches under her fingers and pulls against her skin. It leaves a thin pink mark. She doesn't say anything. K's still grinning, still standing with her arm outstretched.

'I've taken them before so you guys can have a half each for your first time. Look, I'll cut it.'

She puts the pills down next to the sink and presses at one with a nailfile until it cracks. Yasmin reaches out but her fingers only hover above the broken pill. 'I don't know,' she says.

'What do you mean you don't know? You won't die,' says K. She tilts her rum bottle towards Yasmin. 'Take it now.'

Ella already has hers in her mouth and she's bending her face under the tap. She closes her eyes when she swallows. 'Will it take long to work?' she says, wiping her lips on her sleeve.

'Maybe an hour. You'll know. It changes your blood.'

'Are you going to take yours?' says Yasmin. She's back at the mirror combing out her hair. Her half-moon of pill is still there, next to the full one.

'When we get there,' says K.

'Why not now?' says Ella.

'Have to drive.' K pulls off her shirt and the girls notice that she's wearing the bra that boys like. 'I need another drink.' The rum is half done.

'Drive?' says Yasmin.

'Can't we get a taxi? Or the bus?'

'Nah.'

'You can't drive,' says Yasmin.

'Yeah I can.'

'You can't drive.' This time it's forceful. 'Ella, tell her she can't drive.'

Ella rolls her eyes, turns back to the mirror.

'Look, if you don't want to go to the party, just say so. You can get your mum to pick you up. Tell her you feel sick,' says K.

'I don't want to do that,' says Yasmin.

'Well then, we're driving.'

Yasmin taps her comb on her hip. She doesn't argue again.

K takes a tissue to Ella's face, holds her head still with one hand, and pinches at her cheeks. 'You've got too much blush on, you look like a slut.' She pats at the pink film on the fleshy part of Ella's face. There's still that baby fat she hasn't grown out of.

Ella does a tight smile. 'Can you actually drive though?' She says it so Yasmin can't hear.

'Mm, yeah. When Dad's really pissed I go out and move the car a few blocks away and then tell him it's been stolen. So funny.' There's a pile of clothes on the floor and she crouches to pick through them. A pair of her men's underpants are balled in the corner by the door.

'We should get a taxi,' says Yasmin.

'What the fuck is wrong with you,' says K. She's taking off her skirt, standing in just her underwear, a creased dress in one hand and the rum bottle in the other. 'I'm not paying for it. Dad left the car here so I'll drive it. Don't try and stop me.' Her face is motionless and her voice is low. 'I'll fuck up the other side of your face.'

The radio is still playing. Yasmin rubs lipstick off her teeth.

K jerks the mouth of the rum bottle over to Ella. 'One more shot before we go.'

Ella takes a breath and does as she's told. She laughs, and some liquid dribbles out. 'I'm so gross, sorry.'

'Babe, you look great,' says K. She pulls her dress over her head, carefully holds the collar out so she doesn't ruin her make-up.

'Yas, can you zip my dress?' says K. She puts her hand on Yasmin's shoulder. 'I hope you're not mad at me.'

Yasmin has a silly drunk look on her face. 'I'm not mad. Don't be dumb.'

The bulbs in the streetlights are new so it's a floodlit night, a floodlit summer, all lit up like a football game when they walk outside. They hadn't noticed the wind over the sound of their music. The heavy eucalypt branches of the trees in the yard swish at the air. K tosses the car keys up and down, lets them hit the centre of her palm but then she drops them. When she crouches to pick them up the bones in her back jut out, her feet roll from underneath her, and she spills onto the ground.

'Fuck,' she laughs. 'I'm so drunk.'

Ella helps her up.

'I cut my knee.' She shows them a smear of blood on her hand. In the streetlight it looks the most unnatural colour.

'You'll be okay, you'll be right, here's a tissue,' says Ella.

'Do you need to go back inside?' says Yasmin.

'I'm fine, it's funny,' says K. 'Let's get in the car.'

She steadies herself against Ella as they walk out the gate. The three of them have wobbly legs like newborn animals, just babies really. K puts her arm around the girls, like a much older man might do. It's predatory. She unlocks the car for them and nods for them to get in. Yasmin watches as Ella wiggles into the backseat.

'I'm so fucked,' says Ella. 'I'm so drunk,' and she slurs the last word so the sound of it drags on.

It's a big car. K's dad's CDs are alphabetised and stacked neat. The rest of the car is littered with hi-vis work wear and beer bottles that have collected in a heap under the passenger seat. They clink when K drops her bag there.

'Look what I just got,' says Ella. She shows them a text that just says *miss you.*

'That's so cute,' says Yasmin. She doesn't mention anything about Rich being twenty-three. K closes the door and curls onto the front seat. They sit in silence until she speaks.

'Rich won't like your clothes tonight, El, just so you know,' says K.

'What?' Ella's smiling so wide that her eyes are slits. She's wearing a sheer sleeved thing. She rubs her arms.

'He'll think you're ugly. You should try for Benny instead. He likes you.'

'He likes me?'

'Yeah. He'll like you more if you suck his dick, they all do.'

'I've never done that before.'

'At least touch it. Trust me.'

'Can you teach us how?' says Yasmin. There's a new, full bottle of rum nursed in her lap. She twists the plastic seal until it breaks.

The streetlight makes their skin bluish in the dark of the car. Yasmin and Ella's faces are bright from the pills. The three of them laugh madly. Their breath all smells like rum, it's all the same. They grip at each other. K checks her pill is still tucked into her bra.

'I think it's working now,' says Yasmin.

'Yeah the pills are definitely, definitely working,' says Ella.

'I like this,' says Yasmin.

'Good. You can fucking relax now. We're going to have the best night,' says K. She turns to face the road. 'Let's go already. It'll be shit if we're late.'

'You should have got ready faster. You changed twice,' says Ella.

'And if you didn't need so much make-up for that face we would have left like an hour ago,' snaps K. The car keys slip from her fist.

Yasmin bites her mouth, hesitates. 'Why are you such a bitch, Kathleen?'

K snaps around in her seat. 'I'm sorry?' Her face changes. It's twisted with unhappiness.

'I feel very brave right now. Why are you such a bitch? Did we do something to you?' Yasmin tilts her head. She hitches her bra strap back over her shoulder.

Then there is movement. K's hand finds the ends of Yasmin's hair and she yanks at it, then lets go just as fast. Yasmin's mouth hangs wide and Ella has her eyes closed, her arms coming up to cover her chest, some protective instinct.

'You are so ungrateful,' shrieks K. She punches the dash with both fists, over and over. 'Fuck you, you ugly cunt.'

Ella starts laughing nervously. Yasmin, too. 'I was joking, it was a joke. Calm down. You're crazy,' she says.

K waits for her breathing to slow down. 'That wasn't funny,' she says.

'You know we love you,' says Yasmin, draping a hand across K's back.

'Where is this party at again?' says Ella. 'My arms feel good.'

'Pines.'

'Are you sure you can drive?'

K fumbles for the keys on the floor. She sits like her body is built for trouble, her shoulders tensed up, neck forward, mouth set tight against her teeth. Her bare knees are shaking but the girls don't see. She spreads her hands on the wheel, grips it, then lets go. It takes her a few tries to get the keys in the ignition. The car shudders but doesn't start.

LS: Some of my best times have been in bathrooms, getting ready with friends, and I wanted to show a time like that, but with characters with bruising personalities and difficult bonds. When you're very young you'll push yourself to do things so you can stay tight with the people who know you best. I wanted to write about girls who are yet to figure out their place, girls who will mistreat one another as they try to understand how to fit in (or if they'll fit in at all). This is the first story I finished after travelling to Vietnam. It had been through a lot of tense changes, name changes, and remained largely unfinished because I couldn't make it work. I always knew how it ended but it took me a long time to actually write it. I was very uncertain about going to Vietnam. I was worried about my place among the other WrICE fellows; I felt a bit like I didn't deserve to be there. I ended up so lucky to be with people who made it okay to be uncertain. One of the most important things I took away from the fellowship was that my doubts were the same as a lot of people's. It's okay to not know what you're doing, it's okay to abandon a story for a while, or to rework things and change your mind. And all that uncertainty I felt about my work, and about the trip, wasn't the worst thing. It was something that would eventually pass, something that would help me finish this story.

MY TWO MOTHERS

Suchen Christine Lim

'Kwai Chee!'

'What?'

'Will you come back for dinner? I'm going to —'

I shut the door. Cut her off mid-sentence. Didn't bother me that I was rude. I was a teenage pimple on the face of the earth. I wished Yee Ku and Loke Ku hadn't adopted me. I wished somebody else had. Somebody like Miss Lee or Miss Nazareth.

My two mothers were old enough to be my grandmas. They were already in their sixties when I was fourteen.

I can't remember when I started feeling shame about my mothers. It probably began when I was six years old, on my first day of school, in 1958. The other children had a father and a mother. And me? I had Yee Ku and Loke Ku.

Both wore black silk pants and white *samfoo* tops with mandarin collars. Both carried black cloth umbrellas. They shaded me from the sun as we stood in the school field with the other children and their parents. The teachers thought they were maidservants sent by my parents who could not come.

That day I discovered that my two mothers were amah jieh: traditional Chinese domestic servants. They belonged to a sisterhood called the Seven Sisters. They had left their village in southern China in the 1930s to work as amahs in Singapore. I have a black and white photograph of the sisterhood. It shows seven women in matching white samfoo tops and black silk pants, standing in a row. It was taken on the day when they prayed to the Seven Sisters in heaven, plaited their queues, and vowed never to marry.

The Cantonese word *ku* means 'paternal aunt'. But it means more than that in my case. I was their adopted daughter. But I couldn't call either of them 'Mother' because they were unmarried. Two unmarried women living together were my mothers but I *had* to call them 'Aunt' or '*Ku*'. Now you understand why I was confused and angry as a child?

They named me Kwai Chee, or 'Precious Pearl'. But when I went to secondary school, I dropped my Chinese name. I called myself Pearl. It sounded more sophisticated in English.

I told my classmates that my parents had died. I lied that Yee Ku was my grandmother. She had stopped work to bring me up. Loke Ku was our breadwinner. She worked as a live-in maid for a family. She came home once a week to check on us, and once a month, she stayed the night and slept on the same bed with Yee Ku. If I needed to buy anything that cost more than ten dollars, I had to ask Loke Ku. If I failed a test,

I had to answer to Loke Ku. But if I were punished or if I hurt myself, Yee Ku comforted me.

'There, there, don't cry. Big girls don't cry.'

'Ah, Yee, don't spoil her. She's got to learn.'

Loke Ku was the disciplinarian. But I wasn't spoilt. And I did learn. Not love. But shame. A part of me hung my head. I invited no one home. Not because home was a small rented room above a motor workshop in Jalan Besar. More because I felt my family was not normal.

I had two mothers instead of one. Mothers who were unmarried domestics living together. And in the secret chamber of my secretive heart, I suspected them of being something more.

As a child, I couldn't say what it was. It had the faint smell of wrongdoing. Of something that people frowned upon.

How did such an idea enter my head when no one had actually said anything to me? Did I pick things up from the whispers among the neighbours downstairs? From the way they looked at me? Or was it from things that one of my teachers said? Like 'girls should not hold hands', or worse.

I don't know.

I don't know.

I was a confused and angry girl in those days. I was sullen. I studied hard. I buried myself in my books. Not because I enjoyed studying but because I wanted to succeed and leave home. I wanted to get away from the two of them. I was ashamed of myself for feeling that way.

*

In 1965, when I was in the Girl Guides, I met Joyce Lee and Julie Nazareth. They were the adopted daughters of Miss Lee and Miss Nazareth, teachers in Upper Paya Lebar Methodist Girls' School.

Miss Lee, tall and slim, with straight black hair knotted in a bun at the nape of her neck, taught Maths. Miss Nazareth, plump and maternal with a short frizzy brown perm, taught English.

'And you live together as family in the same house?' I asked.

Julie heard the surprise in my voice.

'Ya, we're family.'

Her dark eyes challenged me. I said nothing more. Miss Lee was Chinese. So was Joyce, her adopted daughter, although Joyce looked Eurasian to me. Julie was Indian, like Miss Nazareth. Two single women and their adopted daughters. And they were a family. They lived in the same house, drove to school in one car, and went home together after school was over.

'Anything wrong, Pearl? Why so quiet?'

'Nothing wrong,' I lied.

I was always lying in those days. I couldn't say what was bugging me. At least not straight away. The next Saturday, after our Girl Guides meeting, Julie and Joyce took me home for tea.

'Mummy, this is Pearl,' said Joyce.

'Good afternoon, Miss Lee.'

'Hello, Pearl.'

'And this is my mum,' Julie said.

'Hello, Miss Nazareth,' I said.

Over tea, scones, jam, and *bubur cha-cha*, the conversation somehow got round to family and what a government minister had said in the newspapers.

'That Mr Chan Soo Beng in the Prime Minister's Office. He defines a family as one man, one woman, and their children,' Miss Lee told us.

'Oh yeah, absolutely. People whose parents have died are orphans. Not family, don't you know?'

Miss Nazareth buttered a scone and handed it to me. I couldn't tell if she was serious or joking.

'What about widows, Mum? By his definition, widows and their children are not families then,' Julie said.

'Or … or what about —' Joyce jumped in. 'What about one grandma, one unmarried uncle, and the children of his dead sister? Is that a family?'

'Of course not, silly,' Julie scoffed. 'According to Mr Chan, a family is one man, his wife, and their children!'

'Jeepers, such a broad definition. That should include everybody in Singapore! What about us, Mum?'

There was a pause. Then Miss Nazareth said, 'Some families are born; some families are made.'

'But ours,' Miss Lee looked at Joyce and Julie, 'is specially cooked. We selected our own ingredients.'

We laughed. I caught myself wishing that Miss Lee or Miss Nazareth had adopted me, instead of two illiterate amahs. Class and education clouded my young mind.

*

In 1975, I graduated with a BA (Honours). The night before the ceremony, I put on my gown and hat for Yee Ku and Loke Ku. They were not attending the event.

'You're sure you don't want to come?'

'No need, no need. Just seeing you in your gown and square hat is good enough for us,' Loke Ku said.

I didn't try to persuade them to attend. They would be out of place in the university auditorium.

'Here, Kwai Chee. Let me iron your gown.'

'No, no, Yee Ku, don't fuss. I'll do it myself.'

'Take a taxi tomorrow,' Loke Ku said. 'I'll call for a taxi. Don't rush. Go early.'

'I know. I know. Please. I know what to do.'

They got up early the next morning to offer thanksgiving prayers to the gods. Loke Ku walked me to the taxi stand. Yee Ku, too old and weak by then, stayed at home.

'Yee Ku is cooking your favourite dishes tonight. Abalone soup and stewed mushroom with chicken.'

'Can both of you just stop fussing over me? I don't know what time I can come home. My friends and I are going out to celebrate. After all these years of studying, we need a break!'

I jumped into a taxi and it drove off.

In 2000, years after my two mothers had passed away, I was the writer-in-residence in the University of Iowa.

Laura Jackson, the editor of the university's press, took me home to meet her family. Her partner, Kathleen, was a nurse.

Over dinner, they told me how they had felt something for each other since they were teenagers. In their late twenties, after years of muddled thought and struggle, they had finally committed themselves to each other, with their families' blessings. I thought of my two mothers then and, suddenly, tears came to my eyes.

'A bit of dust,' I said. I caught myself denying them once again — like Saint Peter before the cock's crow.

But that evening, things came full circle for me. I was introduced to Laura and Kathleen's two daughters: Kelly, four, and Sally, three.

'The girls are half-sisters. They share the same biological father.'

I looked from one to the other.

'A very good friend of ours,' Laura said, 'donated his sperm to us.'

'You're pulling my leg.'

'No, we're not,' Laura smiled. 'He even signed an agreement to give up his rights to the girls. I wanted to be a mum real bad. Kathy and I, we wanted a family. So, we asked Carl. He's our best friend. Oh, he's married. Got his own kids. He agreed to help us. One afternoon in the downstairs bedroom, he did what he had to do. I was upstairs, lying in bed, waiting. He handed Kathy the bottle and she syringed his sperm and rushed up the stairs, and squirted it into me.'

'It was a success. Laura gave birth to Kelly,' Kathy said. 'Watching her breastfeed Kelly, I realised that I wanted the experience of giving birth; to be a mother too.'

'One year later, we asked Carl again. My god! We owe that man big!' Laura laughed.

'This time, it was Laura who rushed the syringe upstairs to me.'

'Nine months later, Kathy gave birth to Sally,' Laura added. 'Giving birth to the girls bound us as a family. Kathy stopped work to look after our two daughters.'

'So your daughters have two mothers.'

'She's my Mummy Laura!'

'Mumsy Kathy!'

The two girls shrieked and leapt into their mothers' laps.

'Isn't that wonderful, darling? You've got two mummies to love you.' Laura hugged the girls.

A lump rose in my throat.

'Hmm, well, I … er … I have two mothers too.'

That evening, I did what I couldn't do all those years in Singapore. I told Laura and Kathy about Yee Ku and Loke Ku.

As I talked, my body grew light. My heart expanded. And I saw what I'd failed to see before. Yee Ku and Loke Ku had lived together for more than fifty years. If that wasn't love, commitment, and fidelity, I don't know what is. Theirs was a more lasting relationship than many marriages today. That night, I was proud of them for the first time. And grateful.

Two strangers, unrelated to you by blood, take you into their midst because your parents have died, or don't want you, or are too young or too poor to take care of you. Two strangers take you into their midst and give you a new life. How do you ever say thank you?

*

That night, I remembered them. When Loke Ku came home once a month to stay the night, she would sit in her cane chair on our tiny balcony that overlooked the back lane. Yee Ku would sit in her canvas chair. After dinner, they sat fanning themselves with a palm-leaf fan while I cleared the table. They did not look at each other. They did not speak. But they were connected. An invisible cord bound them as it bound me to them, two old amah jieh, sitting on the balcony above the back lane, insignificant and irrelevant in modern Singapore. Yet this image of them, rising like a pale moon above the rooftops of Jalan Besar, had held me all these years.

I had dinner with Kathleen and Laura several times. They choose to live in Iowa City because the university town recognises their relationship as legal. The church also welcomes them as a family. Iowa City, the city of writers, is an oasis in a hostile desert. The rest of Iowa isn't like this. In Des Moines, the capital, the pastor of a church and his followers burnt the US flag in front of the statehouse when I was there; they wanted to demonstrate their condemnation of gays and lesbians.

Last Christmas, Laura and Kathleen sent me a photo of their family. Kelly and Sally, now aged nine and eight, are in school. And I, the daughter of two mothers, wish them well.

SCL: WrICE Vietnam 2015 was an exhilarating experience, as youth and age, East and West, poets and fiction writers played off and teased one another's imaginations. Every day was a good writing day. There are three iconic Chinese words carved on Hanoi's Pen Tower:

Hsieh Ching Tian ('Write the Clear Sky'). It was as if together we wrote the clear sky, and it is in the spirit of writing the sky that I offer 'My Two Mothers' to the community of readers in Australia and elsewhere. In 2006, I was asked to write a story for the International Women's Day service at the Free Community Church, the only church that served the LGBT community in Singapore. I had never written for or read to this community before this request. On the day of my reading, I was worried. The writer in me felt vulnerable, a feeling I would experience again in the WrICE program when I had to read my unpublished work to a group of writers I had never met before. That Sunday, instead of the usual sermon, I read 'My Two Mothers' to the largely female congregation. The experience was akin to a wonderful cultural exchange that merged the literary with the religious, and I felt deeply honoured by this compassionate community.

M

Amarlie Foster

First reading: For a couple of months after, it seemed every plane fell out of the sky. I was safe — around six thousand kilometres away. Once I looked up the precise distance to store a new number in my head. Otherwise I wasn't sure how I would recover. Basic items like jet lag or replies to any future emails. The bathroom hadn't been cleaned once in my absence. The march of my voice frightened Scott; he scrubbed at the mould invisibly.

I kept my head under the shower. Things were falling out my face. Mouth open above the drain, my heart turning out along with the water. I spoke my name a couple of times down into the hole. When I first arrived, I had put the washing on. At any rate, he was supposed to be on that plane. The one three hundred bodies full. His voice wafted across the sea. I didn't want him then but I wanted to have missed him, the obscene tinyness of those days, made a small movement. I lay in bed until 8.45 to hear the doors slamming in their odd, sensible fashion. Not that the sound shattered inside of me. It was much more about the sweep of air. Some quick intake. Twice a week Scott woke at four to get to work. We slept in separate rooms.

'I read hands expansively, forsaking the details,' the first palm reader had said. He was flexing my left hand with curled fingers. We were going to be on the same flight. My thighs were thick slabs that stuck to the walls of the peninsula any time I exited the hotel. I'd looped my yellow satchel around an ankle; between my knees was the leg of a table. I pushed forward my own legs, sliding and wet with the weather. M was beside me, letting off heat and boredom. The night before, she had whispered to me, *Do you think I'm a bad person?*

'No,' I had answered into the dark. I wanted to go to sleep. The room door opened and shut behind me. We had arrived home separately. M had had too much to drink and her cheeks had taken on this slack manner that made me wince. Watching her climb into the cab like a spring that had lost any tautness, I worried, briefly, that her espousals would spatter onto me, that others on the junket would mentally pair us off together, indefinitely. The palm reader, then beside me, had said the walk was short. I followed him silently down the dirt length beside a highway for sixty-five minutes.

Latest reading: I arrive pointedly. There is a hole in his living-room ceiling and four brown fans stirring. Throughout the reading I exhale again and again and agree with idiotic expanse. His son sits on his lap for some of the time, making grabs at my phone, which is set to record.

'I know about it,' he says, leaning into his child's hair, his voice precise clippings. 'People are always asking two things: will I die early and how many children.'

First reading: I peered over the gap between my arms, and my left hand, the right one slack beside it, ready for the taking. I was thinking about the two plane rides home, attempting to catch sight of my lifeline. He glanced at M's hands, released my own.

'See how much firmer her lines are?' he said. M bent her torso toward him, lazily acquiesced across the distance, made by me, between them; her small hands looped with six rings. Redness crisscrossed her palms.

'This is the one with a strong career — money. Good marriage, just one.'

We mutely considered the junket we were on. No unpleasant stabs; I had good skin. Ten years of dousing myself in tubs of Cetaphil.

'Am I going to die?' I said.

Then his first real movement. He grabbed my hand back. 'Many changes for you, see, no lines?'

He cited astonishment, told me I made my own lines, but he had a voice that didn't seem to catch on anything at all. It was like his skin: waxy, worked over with a butter knife, neat ridges. Smooth and getting along well with time.

'Why don't you complicate your life, no?'

He pulled out a cigarette to demonstrate his point, then lamented no smoking indoors. M joined him outside.

Didi's reading: What else are they supposed to say? I was less pale than usual. I'd never had my palm read but two years earlier Didi had, and I'd watched. Christmas at a bar on Oxford Street, midday, and he'd crouched next to the palm reader, a bushy woman, while I stood beside him in the gloom.

'Twins,' she'd said, and handed back his hand. Then, looking at me: 'But not with you.'

Afterwards, we walked to Glenmore Road. Didi recounted the event to his stepmother, both impressed and hurt by the bushy woman's gall. His stepmother was holding a glass of pink wine with a drunk, sideways look on her face. I laughed at Didi, held onto him. That summer I had developed severe eczema along the lines of three of my left fingers, and rubbed in moisturiser along all the contours of my hands excessively. Elsewhere scars had faded, but the bumps from the eczema remained, changed the fingers' shapes. Didi's cousin, visiting from New York, looked at my marks with disgust and asked if it was contagious. I was passing her a gravy boat. Didi's father threatened to write her out of the will. 'You'll always be their favourite,' Didi said to me last I saw him, Christmas 2013.

First reading: Busying myself on the flight over, I had spotted the palm reader again before I sat down, rows back, and maintained eye contact. Kneeling backwards, turning my pelvis at the last reasonable moment. Decision made. Plane was not turbulent but it shook. I clutched at M's hands. We had different connecting flights.

For five months of 2013 M had slept with a boy named Mop who lived near to my parents in Sydney. We flew up together periodically. We asked passengers to swap seats if we booked separately. As the view of Melbourne fell and was rapidly replaced over and again M said it felt like a rollercoaster, pleased, and squeezed my hands. I hastily looked for omens in the choice of music playing. My childhood friend Laurie would collect us from the airport. In July, Mop ditched M and Laurie was ignoring my texts. We met at a gallery in Chippendale. M looked ugly and bloated when she was unhappy.

'I shouldn't have fucked him,' was all I said, banging my phone against my side. 'I was just bored.'

'You can be really mean,' M said quickly, thinking only of the relationship between she and I.

Here's how it came to be: I had lumbered my overweight, pink suitcase through security, and the palm reader and I farewelled M at the foot of an escalator. She was going north, further into Malaysia. I had one day to waste in Singapore. I followed him, winding my way through an airport bookstore, suitcase trailing. I purchased *This Is the Story of a Happy Marriage*, recommended by M. I had him read my palms again. Same story, no lines. At ten minutes to midnight, we stepped out of a hotel elevator. Level nine, smoker's floor.

'What are you going to do with your life, then?' he said, delaying the farewell.

Announcing the hotel floor were strung two pales full of cigarettes and ash. It struck me that repeating the image ever again would sound like poetic licence. But I had seen it, and never said anything.

'Have children and get married.' I was being laconic.

'That's a shame,' he said, most serious.

An absence of about nine months. What did I do: lay in bed, cooked, got called a whore. My skin grew infected. No longer red dots but yellow pustules; more hair than usual grew on the side of my face. I was moving out of Scott's place in two weeks' time. Things hadn't remained the same. The hotel room felt blanched, like an ice-cream bucket washed out dry and re-used. The door clicked like a container lid. M's grandmother was dead; she was watching my decisions, hawk-like.

I returned from the onsite restaurant, carrying an indiscriminate white plate decorated with watermelons cut into hearts, pineapples into stars. M raised her head from the bed, suspiciously well enough for hopeful eyebrows. Sick from the moment we arrived. Third connecting flight failed to catch. To pass the time for two days I had scrolled the news, waiting to see if untimely sickness turned our deaths averted. A pink suitcase and blue bag making unsupervised chase in Don Muang.

M fucks the same people as I do. Propped up, the only thing we had to watch on my laptop was scattered, ripped episodes of *Girls*. She phrased it: 'Maybe I did it to be an *ass*-hole.'

Then: 'I find it hard to find meaning in someone's art when I do it every day,' M said, pushing her head back into the fat of the pillow, letting the plate slide. I removed it, stared at her. Outside a car backfired, or a heavy load dropped, or a gun went off. I said maybe it was a ceremonial firing of an empty cannon. No planes went down.

Second reading: Barely any stars; blueness. I woke up in time to see the sun. It seeped across the sky, a red certainty advancing. I was writing a report on my time in Singapore. In July, M and I had roamed down King Street, bought tickets to India. For a few months we'd brandished the email confirmation at each other, back and forth. Once I wrote, soothingly, *I actually fly better when I'm alone. It's when I have someone there to let out my anxiety on.*

Then I damaged her. So we spent the first few days in Jaisalmer apart, wandering in the uneventful cold. When we caught sight of each other along a road at sunset, cupping different brands of foreign bottled water, thousands of kilometres were thrown into sharp relief.

'I found her,' M said, irrelevantly.

She had said the morning before: *You should get your palm*

read. It was nearly two years since we had been in Malaysia. *Look, I don't have a love line.* Her eyes were round with forced ignorance.

'No,' I said, not entirely in answer to her. I had hung up as I walked back into our twin-bed hotel room, but M caught the end of the conversation anyway. We had been sanitising our hands obsessively from a small, pink bottle, both afraid of eating. I thought I would write about the bricky weight of unpreparedness, the leash between myself and the oversized suitcase as a metaphor for heady encounters. M always packed appropriately and I didn't. She had been carrying my pink bag on and off again.

'I would never have agreed to this trip had I known there was going to be an invisible third person,' she said, redness spitting out of her mouth. 'I've never seen you like this over anybody. You don't do anything. Everything banks on being with him again.'

'You've never had to manage being away from somebody you love,' I said deliberately, turning to enter the bathroom, flicking the water boiler on with a hotness shooting up my arm. Conversations we'd had about him fired between us. M's face showed rapid accumulation of self-righteous responses; she chose none.

Third reading: Invisible — she wouldn't let me record her speaking. Set on a beige plane: the plan was to break a flight-time record to Adelaide. Nine turbulent hours. President of the United States on board. We were headed backwards, up the centre of Australia. Turned on hidden microphone, lied, was queried, turned the microphone off, lying again. She used a damp towel soaked in alcohol and rubbed at my hand so she could see it better. Grand total of the reading, morphed into something else.

Latest reading: Guess I will write things just exactly how they go. I call him my fiancé; he wants to get his palm read too but for now he is in Melbourne. Before I left, I asked if I could leave a suitcase of books with him. His mother stared at the mass, relieved.

'I'm glad when — have good collections of books,' she said.

Who I am then. I hoped he would find my absence too sluggish to pick up a single one of them. Not assimilate my knowledge. I had boarded the flight as soon as I could, a *who-am-I-kidding* sort of logic. Watched others get seated and click in. I thought about the books and telling him that if I died here he'd need to work twice as hard. But I left it.

Recently I read something along the lines that we do not learn from bad habits, rather spend a lifetime carving away, perfecting them. It was comforting, and so I did the sum of planes and my likelihood of being here again over and over in my head.

For the rest of the trip M and I can only offer each other brief minutes of contentment, like winter suns bleating. We make the walk past Lakshman Jhula but the palm reader requires an appointment, and so we have to wait until five the next day. It puts a halt to the obliging but silent energy between us.

M asks again and again if I can see someone else, in particular a reader in a bursting pink-cement shack on the other side of the Ganges. But *I can't*, I say, and spend the thirty hours until the appointment eating or asleep.

M has clammy palms, this is the truth, a constant that flickers between comic and insulting. She sits adjacent during the reading, says she will *have a go* afterward. *This was your idea*, I tell her in the curves of our bodies avoiding each other as we switch seats. The palm reader calls her dear, and she cuts her eyes to my phone, registering the difference. She is the age I was two years ago. A lifetime of what. I excuse myself to go to the toilet. Weeks later, my fiancé beside me, I pull the string of headphones out from underneath the bed. I skip the recording forward, look to hear myself leaving. At around eleven minutes and however many seconds to go:

'Tendency to stay in the past, kind of depressive,' he is saying. 'But things can be changed, and they do change. If you do change, you decide to go beyond your health problems — stop drinking and this — take a hand imprint one year from now, see the difference. Right? Like I told your friend, she has anxiety problems. But if she started doing some sort of boxing ...' There was a pause. 'Masculine sports. She would sleep better.'

And,

'Any of your relationships, if they end, it won't be any kind of fighting, shouting. Not these kinds of affairs. It will end very nicely, peacefully. If it does. If you need it to end.'

First reading: On advice of M I have taken to recording certain conversations. A blue duffle coat, microphone on in one pocket. The palm reader says, *You're very aggressive.*

'No, I'm not, I'm anxious,' I say. We are alone.

He looks at me, softness and hardness rearranging themselves, a blank slate making silent impressions. The hotel window looks out on vast concrete and so he wanted the blinds closed. (Fiancé in my own bed, the new curtains pulled shut every time he arrives. People can see us. / I've lived here a year, they can't. / If you can see them, they can see you.) There is an empty tennis court too, I point out to the palm reader. I pull the beads the wrong way before the right way. The weight clinks against the glass.

In the playback you can hear one sock taking slightly longer than the other to pad against the carpet. Another sound: 'You are aggressive. You should take up boxing.'

Second reading: 'Was that what you wanted?' M said, the yellow of the day established. It was the first time she had spoken that morning.

During the reading she had mouthed her dissent when the woman told me I would have one good marriage. The palm reader had been middle-aged; she asked me to play back the recording once she discovered the microphone was on. But it was only so she could hear her own voice for the first time.

Now M and I were next to the oldest cannon in India, or so the sign was written. Hard to say. I was perched on a staircase while M was below, hands surveying the view and her hips.

'You've got to leave it, like crockery,' M continued, pointing to the almost-dry muck of henna that I was tracing with my other hand, removing the hardened edges. It occurred to me. A photo snapped at Singapore airport, my face turned similarly downwards, avoiding the lights. I hadn't taken the pink suitcase at all, but a small, brown one. The pink one was still in a wardrobe in Melbourne, stuffed with clothes.

'That's where we've got to go,' M said, pointing to another yellow lookout, obscured. It seemed to me M's assertions had shifted. Now was only the thinnest mask of appearing invested in where she was. It was so lazy I wondered if she was provoking me. I ignored her.

'Yeah, that's ...' I read the sign on the wall, tired. 'Famous.'

'For what?'

'Its rings. I read about it. Online. It's a jewellery shop.'

'Did you want to go?' she said.

'Yeah.' I didn't know what else to do. There were three more planes between my fiancé and me.

'Give me your hand, not that one,' M said, and laughed without anything behind it. To her, Jaisalmer was weightless. I stood, two ledges above, ignoring her outstretched palm.

AF: During my stay in Penang I happened to have my palm read while waiting for a cab. The collection of poetry I went on to write tracked a woman who fell in love with a palm reader and chased him around the globe. I have had my palm read a few more times since. The verdicts have all been unanimous. Of the twelve writers I spent my ten WrICE days with, half identified as poets. At the time, this surprised me. The experience altered the course of my practice. It was certainly a romantic introduction — smoky nights in back rooms with lone trumpet players, and poetry that moved from English to Malay. Since then, my writing has tended to come out roughly fifty-fifty between short fiction and poetry. 'M' is a remodelling of a suite of poetry I wrote in the year following my fellowship. It was my first-ever attempt to delve into writing poetry. Prior to this, I had barely raised my head over the wall of short fiction to see what any other style of writing looked like. 'M' is somewhere between new fiction, a reviving of the poetry, and a sketch of my history with palm reading. It has retained a certain strange elusiveness but, I hope, manages coherence.

THE ILLOI OF KANTIMERAL

Alvin Pang

Having lost her vada to the sea, she kept watch every dawn on the beach where she had last caught sight of him, adrift in his skoyak midway between shore and horizon. Every morning at the third ori, before the sun called the world to its labours, she would add a piece of dried kan to her rice phut in an oiled nanal leaf and depart the house without waking chibu, who would more often than not be slumped over her worktable in the smaller inner room of the house, the one with the broken window.

The small path that wound around the cliff edge, wide enough only for one person to pass, was dewy and treacherous in the dark, but soon opened onto a sandy crescent, bound to the north and south by two ancient breakwaters. It was to the one farther off, which the villagers called *davada meral*, grandfather of the coast, that she would make her way, clutching her breakfast as she clambered over the slippery rock to the narrow but sturdy plateau.

She would eat with both hands, all the while scanning the horizon for signs of life, quickly spotting then looking past the lurelights of the sotokan boats and the dim red glow of the jhimcatchers. The flipper of a passing bhaphaun would appear for a moment to be a human arm, waving in greeting or distress. On occasion a uluabird skimming the surface of the water would take the shape of a distant boat, its one raised wing like a soksail unfurled to catch the shorebound wind.

It never seemed to rain while she was keeping watch, or if it did she took no notice, her feet firmly lodged in the crevices of the elder breakwater. Before long the sun would pry the horizon open with golden fingers and the sea would begin to gleam the colour of wet jade.

Climbing down from the breakwaters, she would fold her nalal leaf into a little skoyak, leave inside it one last bite of kan and rice, set it afloat where the tug of the waves was gentle but steady, and walk away from the makeshift boat without looking back, as she returned home to her chores.

Have you eaten, chibu would ask as she came through the door.

Yes, she would reply, *and so has vada.*

Then come help me with the morning offering, nurlin, before you go and check the nets.

Yes, chibu.

And she would immerse herself in the day's work until nightfall and sleep.

*

The villagers were all aware of her morning vigil. *Everybody knows your vada has run away to the mainland,* the nurlins and erlins would tease whenever she came to the village market. *He is the best illukan catcher on the coast, and some big-brana porneu has hooked him for herself.*

The village matrons would give her knowing looks, but not once did they offer a word of comfort or advice. Instead, they fussed among themselves to be the first in line at her stall, for she seemed to have her vada's knack of always having the freshest, biggest catch of the day for sale.

Once in a while, one of the erlins her age would come to sit with her on the breakwater before dawn. One of them brought her a stolen container of sweet koomi, which his dabu had fermented, skimmed, and filtered under the full moon just the night before. In silence, she and the erlin watched the lunar tide swell and foam. The next night, she readied an extra portion of kaniphut for him, but he did not come that dawn or the next, or the one after. Later she found out that his drowned body had been found in a nearby cove, nibbled at by the sea's remorseless denizens, a half-drunk canister of koomi still strapped to his waist.

The next dawn, she made sure to set aside an extra morsel in her skoyak offering to the sea.

She was sixteen when the dark-haired erbo came to her, adorned with the seaglass bracelets, earrings, and leather skirts of a Mayar's heir from the neighbouring Johrikanti. Without asking for her leave, he sat down cross-legged next to her.

You are indeed very pretty, said the Johribo, who had come to the island to negotiate passage and trade. *The villagers spoke of a mysterious beauty who appears every dawn on this rock, and now I see they spoke truly.*

She had never thought of herself as beautiful. Big-boned and ample like her vada, her cheeks were flat, her lips thin, her hair a tangled pukk of dirty straw, her arms grown stout from years of pulling at the nets. Still, her eyes were clear and bright, and she cut a comely figure in the pre-dawn gloom. So she remained silent, and watched the sea.

I do not know whether you are a sea-fairy, one of the illoi, he continued, *but even if you were —*

He took her left hand in his, placed within it a large pearl, and closed her fingers over it —

So fine and magnificent a treasure should tame you.

She felt the cool, hard sphere press into her palm. *Now*, he said, *tell me your name.*

I have no name, she replied. *My vada disappeared, before he could give me one, as is our custom.*

Ah, so have you been waiting all this time for him to come back and name you? Do not trouble yourself. Let me give one to you now.

He kissed her, and pressed her against the sea-moist granite for what seemed a long time. When she came to her senses, he was gone. The sun had risen a hand's width into the sky, the skraws had begun their first hunt, and the rock was stained with her blood.

*

The next night, she armed herself with her vada's old kantoo, which over the years she had kept sharp enough to scale and gut a kan without leaving the visible line of a wound. But the dark-haired erbo did not come, nor was she certain what she would do if he did. Her vigil, for the first time, felt a lonesome one, and she clutched her vada's blade for assurance.

When dawn arrived, she let fall two fresh drops of her blood onto the little skoyak offering and watched the tide carry it out beyond sight, before turning at last towards home.

Her discovery that she was pregnant did not deter her from her daily ritual. Hours after giving birth to her erlin, she made her way to the shore with him at her breast, tucked away from the night chill, and dabbed his dark forelocks with saltwater before taking up her watch. Before long she had prepared two portions of breakfast and crafted two nanal skoyaks, as her erlin scratched and tossed about in the nearby sand in the darkness, nameless and unafraid.

Chibu said that the Johribo, the Mayar's erlin who had now become Mayar, had come to their house one afternoon, having heard of her child, assuming it to be his. He would call again soon to fetch both nibu and erlin, to be formally installed as part of his extended household.

That day she took her finest illukan, which spends its time in the depths and never sees daylight but has the sweetest flesh, and cleaned it fit for a Mayar's table. Into one of its large eye sockets she inserted the pearl he had given her, its lustre matching perfectly the illukan's intact, deep-seeking eye.

Into its gullet she placed her erlin's pacid, carefully preserved in bohoil since his birth. Then she seasoned and wrapped the dish in nanal, and asked for it to be given to the Joharibo when he came. She left the house to tend to her nets with her erlin in tow.

The gift was received, a small token was left behind in acknowledgement, and the Johri Mayar never again returned to village, sending envoys instead whenever there was business to be conducted.

In time she became dabu, and later tydabu, but she was never too frail to climb the breakwater every dawn; and if the effort required the assistance of a walking cik and a few willing erlins, none thought to speak against it. Kancatchers and meribos, as they headed out to sea or returned from a night's hunt, would try to spot her silhouette for good luck, and the sight of her would steady them, even if the waters happened to be troubled that dawn.

After her passing, the villagers placed a driftwood monument on the old breakwater, shaped like a sitting nuebo, her arms outstretched and watching the sea. For years, although no one in the village had agreed or made plans to do so, a kanlam would be kept lit at the monument, from the third ori until dawn, always visible midway between the horizon and the shore.

Did she ever reveal why she kept that vigil every morning?
Surely she realised her father would not be coming home?

I suppose it began as a kind of grieving, and then became habit. Probably she found her own peace in the routine; time to be quiet and to think. Watching the sea was the one thing she could call her own, that was not hers by right or responsibility. It taught her a way of being in the world that was hers alone.

As a child my own vada used to keep her company sometimes, up on that stretch of rock. He said she preferred not to speak a word until it was time to leave, but on the walk home she would tell him stories about the things she had seen while on watch. The flight of bright-winged dhuokan in hunting formation. A forsaken nuebo who had tried to drown herself and her unborn chilin in the darkness, but was startled by a piece of shale tossed in her direction and changed her mind. Mysterious lights coming from the ruined sky-towers on the far end of the coast, near the great fallen city of which they say we were once a district. And her own tale, of course: that is how we know to tell it.

So she never did have a name. How did she even manage?
And what about her son?

Oh, she had many names. In the stories that have been told of her, she has been called different things, not all of them pleasant. But there was never any doubt what she meant to us. She was the most respected kantookay of the village, and tybo of the marketplace. She was nibu to her erlin, and dabu to his children, and tydabu to us all. And of course she was always nurlin and chilin to her chibu.

Did you know that *chibu* in the Kantiyan tongue means 'mother of the heart'? The term for 'birthmother' is *nibu*, and it was considered a step less intimate than a woman of no relation who had freely taken up the duty of caring for a child who had been orphaned or cast aside. One had to earn that name, and it was never given without love.

Her erlin, our davada, she named *Tilyak*, once he came of age. It means 'received'. Most people think she was referring to the trinket left behind by the Johribo who was our tydavad, because that's what such tokens are called in the language of trade. A kind of receipt. Then again, she always spoke about having received many gifts from the sea in the long years of her watch, so she might also have been thinking of her erlin in that way.

You need to understand, we do not just pick our names out of a dook, with no regard for what we are or may become. When she passed the village had to decide what to inscribe on her grumu. But she had thought of that too. In her hand, on her deathbed, she was clutching — this.

It looks like a tiny carved fish.

In the Kantiyan tongue, the words for 'island' and 'fish' are one and the same, which is why we islanders are also called the Fish People. This is the symbol for an island. There were many such carvings, each indicating a word, and each word linked to a legend. Synga, the lion and the lost city. Nung, the mountain and how it once shed blood tears. Umi, the sea urchin, who showed lovers where to meet on the hidden beach that only appears at nip tide. These ikoglyphs were meant to be strung together and dangled from a belt or worn as a bracelet, like a good-luck charm. They were very popular at the time, and were often exchanged as tokens of goodwill.

This was part of the trinket left to her by the Mayar.

Yes, but look at the carving she chose out of the set. The island glyph is the only one that is connected with a song instead of a tale. It is never written down, but every nurlin and erlin on the coast knows it by heart before they learn to swim. It is about remembering and forgetting and the tide of time. In the modern script, the refrain would go something like this: *yan kan tibi po meri tanti si.*

'We are islands … '
… but the sea is whole.

AP: 'The Illoi of Kantimeral' began as a chance encounter with an old writer friend whom I had not seen in years, at a conference in Cebu, Philippines. During a trip out to sea, I saw her scanning the coastline for indications of an old beach hotel to which her father, also a well-known author, had brought her as a child on one of his literary sojourns.

This remarkable quest, along with our encounter after so many years, must have taken root — upon my return to Singapore, I drove out to the beach soon after and wrote this in one swift flurry. The story is set in an imagined distant future in which the grand urban trappings of modern Singapore have once again fallen into history (as so many cities have in our region's past). It features terms from an invented language, Kantiyan, that I imagine to be a plausible descendant of the many languages and cultures that already infuse Singapore and South-East Asia — including English, Malay, Portuguese, Spanish, and the Chinese tongues; the words may sound half-familiar to speakers of these languages. Their precise meanings may or may not be immediately discernible from context, but neither is the experience of engagement, negotiation, resistance, and mystery within the Asia-Pacific itself as straightforward as we might wish the world to be. There is humility and pleasure in earnest encounter, and in listening out for the inherent humanity of what we do not fully recognise. I shared this story at the inaugural WrICE residency in Penang both as a way to gather views about whether the milieu of the story might be extended, as well as to honour the inclusive, pan-cultural spirit of the WrICE project.

TRAMPOLINE

Joe Rubbo

When we get home from school my brother's dad, Jerry, is out the front, leaning against a truck that has a trampoline strapped to the back of it. He's holding a cigarette between thumb and forefinger, the burning tip disappearing into his cupped hand. As we pull into the driveway, he takes one last drag, drops the butt to the road, and crushes it with the heel of his boot. There are two guys I've never seen before sitting on the nature strip, one of them chugging down a carton of iced coffee.

Mum yanks up the parking brake and we all sit there listening to the engine tick over. No one says anything. The car is starting to heat up now the air conditioning's shut off. I can feel my thighs suctioning to the seat. Mum billows her shirt with pinched fingers and blows the hair off her face. After a while she says to my brother, 'Do you know what your dad's doing here?'

Justin picks at the vinyl flaking away on the door handle. 'Nup.'

'He's giving you a trampoline, by the looks of it,' Mum says, taking the keys out of the ignition and holding them in her fist.

Jerry is still standing over by the truck, his head cocked to one side like he can't work out what the problem is. His face is scrunched up hard against the sun. I wave at him, but I don't think he sees me because he doesn't wave back.

'You know about this?' Mum says.

Justin looks at her, tongue wiggling the silver stud below his lip. 'Nup.'

'Bullshit, Justin. You could've given me some warning.'

'I didn't know about it. I don't even want a trampoline.'

'I do,' I say, sticking my head between their seats. 'I want a trampoline.'

They both ignore me.

'Jesus, I'm starting to cook in here,' Mum says, cracking the door. 'You better go and say hello.'

Justin gets out of the car and walks over to Jerry, his thumbs hooked underneath his backpack straps. Jerry punches him in the arm and Justin shrugs away. They both stand there looking at each other. The two men I don't know get up off the nature strip and brush the dry grass from their jeans.

Me and Mum go round the back of the car and she pops the boot, which lets out a fart of banana-scented heat. She gives me a couple bags of shopping and takes all the others herself.

'Jerry,' she yells, slamming the boot shut with her elbow. 'Don't even think about it.'

Jerry just waves back at her, smiling.

'And pick up your bloody cigarette butt.'

I follow Mum through the front gate.

'If he wants to put it in the backyard,' I say, 'then you should let him.'

'Is that right?' she says, kicking the gate shut behind me.

Nintendo is crouched behind his kennel, strings of saliva hanging from his mouth. When we get close he darts out and starts running rings around Mum, his nails scraping against the brickwork. Mum pushes him away with the toe of her shoe. He comes at me next and I swing the shopping bags until one of them, heavy with tins of baked beans, hits him in his side. He yelps and scuttles off back behind his kennel.

'Bloody Jerry,' Mum says, opening the front door.

'He's all right.'

'What would you know about it?'

We go inside and I kick off my shoes so I can feel the slate tiles, cool against my feet.

'He can do a Rubik's Cube without looking it up on YouTube,' I say.

Mum laughs. 'That's because he doesn't have a job.'

'He brought us a trampoline. That's good.'

'Good example of him being a dickhead, more like.'

We dump the shopping on the bench and Mum starts going through the bags, looking for the Viennetta. She pulls it out of a bag and pushes it sideways into the freezer and then starts putting away the rest of the shopping. I get myself a juice box from the fridge and punch in the straw.

'That bloody game,' she says, head in the pantry. 'Now this.'

She's talking about the arcade machine, Jerry's last present for Justin. It's one of those real old ones — takes up nearly a quarter of Justin's room and it only has *Space Invaders* on it. He still makes me pay twenty cents every time I want to play.

'Jerry likes big presents.'

'Jerry likes to be an inconvenience.'

'Why's that?'

'Shit, I don't know. Can you see if the dog's got water?'

'Yep.'

But instead I go into my dad's study and pull up the blinds so I can see what's going on out in the street. They've untied all the ropes holding the trampoline in place. Jerry is standing up on the truck, while the other guys are down on the street. They lower it down slowly. Jerry's face is deep red, the veins in his neck bulging blue, and I can see the sweat pouring off him from here. The other guys don't seem all that bothered. Justin's sitting on the kerb, both thumbs poking his mobile phone.

Once they've got the trampoline on the road, Jerry stands there with his hands on his waist, breathing hard. Then, when Jerry's ready, they hoist the trampoline up off the road and shuffle over towards the house. I can hear Jerry swearing from here.

I go back into the kitchen and wait for them to come around the side, standing by the window and sucking at my juice box until I hit air.

'Did you water the dog?' Mum asks.

Nintendo is cutting sick, running in circles and nipping at the men as they walk across the garden.

'Robyn,' Jerry yells, loud enough for us to hear him through the glass. 'Do something about this dog, would you?'

Mum doesn't look up from chopping carrots. 'We need to get a bigger dog,' she says, not really to me. 'One that bites more than just feet and ankles.'

'Like a German Shepherd?'

Mum gives me the look that tells me it's time to stop talking.

They put the trampoline in the corner of the backyard, right next to the fat palm tree. Jerry shakes hands with one of the men and then they slouch towards the driveway. I can hear the truck grinding through the gears as they drive off. The trampoline covers most of the lawn.

Jerry comes over and opens the kitchen door. He only sticks his head in.

'So,' he says, 'how about that?'

Mum keeps chopping, her knife thudding harder and harder into the board.

'Pretty rad,' I say.

'I guess you're not happy about it.'

'Fuck off, Jerry.'

'Fair enough.'

Justin comes in, drops himself onto the couch, and turns on the TV. Bear Grylls is on the screen, shirtless and shivering by a lake. His lips are bright blue and he's talking at the camera about the importance of keeping warm.

'Is that it?' Mum says to Jerry.

'Unless you're going to invite me to stay for dinner.'

'Ha!'

'Just,' Jerry says, 'aren't you going to give her a bounce?'

'Maybe later.'

'I will,' I say.

Jerry winks at me. 'Well, I better head off.'

'Bye, Jerry,' I say.

Mum and Justin don't say anything.

'Justin, I'm gonna get going.'

'Yeah, bye, Dad.'

Jerry hangs there a little longer, looking at Justin. He taps the door handle with the heel of his palm and says, 'OK.'

He closes the door and walks back around the side, all the time looking at the trampoline like he built it or something. Mum doesn't watch him go. She gathers up most of the sticks of celery, carrot, and cucumber and puts them into Tupperware containers. The rest she puts on a plate, which she slides over the kitchen bench towards me.

'Eat these. Now.'

I climb up onto the stool, pick up a celery stick, and watch Mum as she scoops up the bright curls of vegetable peel from the bench and dumps them into the bin. She stops by the sink and looks at the trampoline, its shadow sliding across the lawn.

'Fucking cunt,' she says.

'I heard that,' Justin says.

'Is there any peanut butter?' I say, holding up the finger of celery.

*

Me and Mum have a bet going. See how long it takes Dad to notice the trampoline. I say next week. She says never. But he surprises us both by noticing it that night over dinner. I guess it is almost the only thing you can see when you look out the glass doors next to the dining table.

'Pretty big,' he says, folding the newspaper and tucking it under his elbow.

'Yep,' Mum says.

'You boys must be happy.'

I nod. Justin doesn't look up from his plate.

'Didn't he get you that thingo once?' Dad says, pointing his fork at Justin.

'*Space Invaders* machine,' I say.

'Yeah,' Dad says.

'Yeah,' Justin says.

Dad laughs. 'What's Jerry doing, looting theme parks or something?'

'I don't see why he can't just give me cash,' Justin says.

'Hear, hear,' Mum says.

'Cash is the last thing you'll ever get from Jerry,' Dad says. Mum cuts him a look. 'Not now.'

'Did Jerry tell you how the dogs are going?' Dad asks.

'Leave him alone,' Mum says, forking some salad into her mouth and looking at Justin.

But Dad has to re-tell the story about Jerry and his venture into greyhound racing, even though we've all heard it a million times. There's no stopping him now that he's gotten started. It's his favourite Jerry story at the moment.

A few months ago, Jerry showed up with a racing dog he called Mixed Harmony. He used to keep her at a kennel near Kinglake. On Black Saturday, Jerry and his friends drove out to see how Mixed Harmony was coming along, somehow clueless to the fact there was a pretty serious bushfire shaping up. By the time they got to the kennels it was starting to get scary and the trainer had already started herding all the dogs onto a truck.

He was furious when he saw Jerry and his mates pull up, told them to get lost. They'd driven over two hours in the scorching heat just to see her. But Jerry didn't mind. In that short time, he'd already gotten all he wanted out of the trip. As the dogs were moving across the yard, something seemed to startle them and they started running towards the truck, their long bodies low to the ground as they picked up speed. Jerry had stood by the car a moment, hills burning around him, and watched Mixed Harmony kick out wide of the pack. She'd started near the back, but made up ground quick. The way Jerry described it, the whole world seemed to slow down except for Mixed Harmony. 'First up the ramp,' he told us, excited. 'And that's against some real champions.'

But Mixed Harmony never even made it onto the track. She was too skittish. Jerry felt obliged to take her on as a pet. He calls her Harm for short.

'You couldn't invent it,' Dad says.

'Yeah, yeah,' Mum says. 'Laugh it up.'

'He told me he's met someone,' Justin says, squashing peas with the back of his fork. 'Reckons he's in love.'

Mum snorts. 'Yeah, right.'

'He's moving to Broome to be with her, says she's going to get him a job on a pearl farm.'

Mum puts down her knife and fork. The sounds of cicadas fill up the silence.

'Well,' Dad says after a while, 'good for Jerry. I'm sure Harm will appreciate the warmer weather. Always cold, greyhounds.'

After the plates are cleared, Mum brings out the Viennetta and puts it in front of Justin. There are fourteen candles sticking out of it.

'You forgot one,' I say.

Mum crosses her arms. 'They come in packs of seven.'

'Don't you dare sing,' Justin says.

Dad looks at Justin. 'Is it your birthday, mate?'

After dinner I go out to the trampoline. It isn't like my friend Ben Keenan's — those ones with the tightly woven black material that don't give up much bounce. This one is bigger by half. The bed is blue and there's a faded red cross in the middle. The springs are fatter than my forearms. I clamber up and the crosshatched material pinches at my bare feet.

The trampoline sends me up high and straight. In the air, it's like I've got a couple of minutes to do whatever the hell I want. I run through all the tricks I know. Bum, back, and belly drops. Front flips. Backflips. Three-eighties, arms helicoptering around me.

At my highest I can see all the tennis balls stuck on our roof, my head almost touching the palm fronds. Nintendo watches me the whole time from behind the paperbark tree, ears flat, tongue hanging out.

After a while the Viennetta feels like it might come out of me so I stop bouncing and sit down. The trampoline cradles my bum. The sun drops behind the next door neighbour's prickly pears and the garden turns a dark green.

I lie back and look up. The blue in the sky is giving way to black. Stars are starting to punch through. It's then, running my hand over the trampoline, that I feel it. A rough patch.

I kneel close to inspect it. One of the threads has come loose. There's a hole in the very centre of the cross. But then, the hole isn't very big at all. I can just wiggle two fingers through to the other side.

JR: This piece couldn't be much further from Vietnam. But that is where I wrote it: sitting at a small coffee table in my room at the Long Life Riverside Hotel, the fan rattling overhead. I could hear the water lapping against the edge of the pool and the voices of the hotel staff, the clicks and cadences of the local tongue. Just outside the hotel was the town of Hoi An, and beyond the town, the rice paddies criss-crossed with roads. But there I was, sequestered away in my room, writing a short story set in the suburban Australia of my childhood. In some ways it felt like cheating, or perhaps not getting the most out of the experience. I wasn't immersing myself. The opposite. I was removing myself from this many-textured place, trying to shut out its distractions. All this changed when we came together in the late afternoon to read our work. I heard stories from places far and close, by new friends. In these moments, as they read their stories, other worlds came rushing in. When it came time for me to read, this story felt right. A small story of family life. A refraction of the world I came from.

STANDING IN THE EYES
OF THE WORLD

Bernice Chauly

Kuala Lumpur. KL. *Kala Lumpa* or *Kala Lampur* to the white man, the Mat Sallehs. City of sinners and sex. Sodom and Gomorrah. It was 1998, and the city was *partay central* of Asia. Of the world. Drugs had opened up the minds of this one-time placid society. Drugs had bayed in a new revolution, in a time where people hungered for freedom from authoritarian politicians, from the police, from their mindless jobs, from themselves.

Ecstasy had hit the town, in a way that could only be described as monumental. There were *feng tau* clubs in Bukit Bintang, Cheras, and Jinjang that catered to the Chinese riffraff, the Ah Bengs and Ah Lians who felt ill at ease in the posh, uppity bars like Museum and the Backroom Club.

There were clubs for Indian gangsters in Sentul and Selayang; there were dodgy *dangdut* clubs on Jalan Ipoh and

Brickfields, where the girls would dance with you, get high with you, and then go down on you; there were underground clubs that opened up after the other ones closed, then stayed open till people had come down from their highs.

Dealers were raking it in. MDMA was on everyone's lips and tongues. There was pussy and dick everywhere. White. Brown. Yellow. Black.

Everybody was high.

DJs flew in from all over the world to play to hundreds, thousands of people who swallowed pink, blue, white pills. E. Everybody wanted E. Nobody drank alcohol; water was the salve for the days and nights on sweaty dance floors.

Ecstasy was prayer. Ecstasy was the new God.

The Asian financial crisis was crawling out. Billions were lost, millions gained. The ringgit had been pegged at 3.80 against the US dollar. It saved us. Our other ASEAN neighbours didn't fare as well.

The Petronas Twin Towers were finally complete. The towering phallic monstrosities had transformed the city. And there were stories that bled upon storeys for fodder. It was the topic of conversation at every dinner table, every *mamak* stall, every *kopitiam* between Bangsar and Cheras, how ugly it looked. How sterile, how un-KL, how Western.

Aiyo, so sci-fi.
Like Gotham City.
So ugly wan.
Celaka betul.
'Cursed'. Cursed to never be built.

Before the Towers, the site was a racecourse. Built by the British because they knew the land was unsafe for any structure taller than a coconut tree. That underneath the turf was a network of limestone caves. To build the world's tallest twin structures above a hollow catacomb of caves was an act of folly, of utter stupidity. It was a disaster in the making. Mahathir's 'twin pricks', that's what it was. A sign that Malaysia had come into its own. That 'we' had arrived. That our quest to have the world's tallest flagpole, its longest beef murtabak, and the biggest mall in Asia had succeeded — and that Malaysians had something, finally, something, to be proud of.

These towers, designed by a New Yorker of Argentinean descent and built by rival Japanese and Korean engineering companies who had to pump millions upon millions of tonnes of concrete into miles of limestone caves, had validated our feeling that Malaysia had arrived. Never mind that thousands of Bangladeshi and Indonesian workers, who had slaved away on meagre wages, and who were crushed to death in hushed-up accidents, had built it. That they'd died senselessly like frogs, *mati-katak*, for another notch in our country's race to become a First World nation by 'looking' like a First World nation.

The towers loomed over KL, a new symbol for the city, like the Sears Tower, like the Empire State Building. We had come to be defined by two eighty-eight-storey shards of concrete, aluminum, glass, and steel. Two towering hexagons, inspired by sacred Islamic geometry, of course. From distant suburbs to the Golden Triangle, the Twin Towers rose above everything else, flanked by the KL Tower, now dwarfed and comical with its pink shaft. This was engineering at its best, this was the strongest steel in the world, capable of withstanding tremors, where steel beams could bend under pressure.

It was a memorial for all those who'd died.

It was haunted, of course, like every other building in KL. The ghosts of the fallen would never be venerated here. Instead, people would flock to Gucci, Bally, Prada, British India, and Aseana to proselytise to the gods of haute couture.

The newly built Bukit Jalil Sports Complex was sprawled out and ready for the Commonwealth Games. Malaysians were gearing up for the world stage, our time had come to show the world that we were capable, that *Malaysia Boleh*! Yes, we can! That we had arrived.

In September, everything changed.

On 2 September, Malaysia's Deputy Prime Minister, Anwar Ibrahim, was sacked by Mahathir Mohamad, the dictatorial, authoritarian Prime Minister who had ruled for seventeen years.

On 11 September, the Commonwealth Games opened with no-expense-spared pomp, fireworks, and circumstance. Ella, the pint-sized Malaysian songstress, performed the theme song of the games, 'Standing in the Eyes of the World', in smouldering black eyeliner and with poor diction.

I hope you enjois! ... to screaming multitudes.

On 20 September, Anwar Ibrahim was arrested.

On 29 September, he appeared in court with a black eye.

Malaysia, the beloved country of my birth, would never be the same again.

*

Run!

   The gas is coming again!
   The mosque!
   Get into the mosque!

We ran, like thousands of crazed rats trying to dodge each other. Our clothes were drenched and I realised immediately that it was impossible to run effectively with soggy shoes. My hand automatically covered my camera lens. *A wet lens was a dead lens.* My feet slipped and slid inside my drenched sneakers, threatening a twisted ankle. I did not need or want a sprain or a broken limb. Mira grabbed my hand, her eyes wild.

   Are you OK?

I nodded. Our slippery hands held fast. I heard screams as some tried to rub the tear gas from their eyes, giving in to instinct. There was nothing like tear gas to make you angry. Politicise you. Our politicians had no idea what they were doing. Revolutionaries were created on the street, that very day.

   The protest took place a few hours before Anwar's arrest. We had gathered outside the National Mosque, getting handphone messages saying he was going to be there. I picked Mira up from her apartment in Sri Petaling and we drove into the city. The traffic was bumper-to-bumper all the way from Jalan Parlimen; cars were inched up against each other and we snaked along the road, all the way to Dataran Merdeka, Independence Square. A detour towards Central Market enabled us to find a spot in the parking lot. There were thousands of people already walking towards the mosque. You could sense the excitement, the anger. It was brittle, electrifying.

Anwar was sacked for supposed sexual misconduct — specifically, adultery and sodomy. In a country where draconian laws still harked back to the time of the British, giving someone a blow job or having anal sex was a heinous crime.

The daily newspapers barked out offensive headline after offensive headline, demonising Anwar.

Sodomite! Adulterer! The Rise and Fall of Anwar Ibrahim.

These words unleashed a national fury and Malaysians of all ages took to the streets. It was Reformasi. The Malaysian Reformation had begun.

Mahathir's regime had created a generation of Malaysians who were complicit and afraid. The Internal Security Act ensured that. Detention without trial. Guilty until proven innocent. You were always guilty. Even if you weren't.

Mira was angry. We all were. She had studied law in the UK and we'd both been writers at *The Review* — 'the smartest men's magazine in town' — for two years. We had liked each other from the start, we understood each other. We liked to drink and talk. We knew that what was happening was historic. And that it would change us forever.

By the time we got to the mosque, we could barely see Anwar, who was perched on a makeshift podium. We could only hear the hailer. I started taking pictures. All around me, I saw angry faces. Twisted and with anger.

Let them do their job! The media is showing us who they really are: dogs! Anjing! Liars! Penipu! They supported me and now they want to see me guilty. Guilty! Do you think I am guilty?

The crowd roared. I heard fifty thousand voices, all shouting in unison.

No! HE is guilty!

Allahu Akbar! Allahu Akbar!

Together our fists rose in solidarity.

'We who are gathered here in Kuala Lumpur pledge to defend the freedom and sanctity of the nation to the last drop of our blood ... we resolve to revive the spirit of freedom ... we will not suffer injustice and oppression in the land ... we will not suffer the replacement of foreign oppressors with those raised from among ourselves ... we oppose all cruel and oppressive laws which deny the people their fundamental rights and freedoms ... we denounce those who corrupt our system of justice ... we denounce corruption, abuse of power, and the conspiracy devised by a greedy elite to blind the people to the truth in order to maintain their grip on power and wealth.'

The crowd roared.

Reformasi! Reformasi!

Anwar, voice hoarse and fist raised, continued.

'We raise the spirit of freedom! We are united against oppression! We are united in our resolve to establish justice! Long live the people! Give victory to Reform! We demand the resignation of Mahathir Mohamad!'

Mira and I looked at each other. We grinned widely.

The revolution has begun.

Behind us, the Federal Reserve Unit trucks rolled up and the clanging started.

As if out of politeness, a bell rang three times. And then

the jets of water hit us like a torrent of stones. A merciless pounding. Water bullets. We were getting a beating.

We screamed. The water was ferocious. I fell against a man behind me. He fell against someone else and together we tumbled to the ground like tiddlywinks. Arms, legs, hair, everywhere. All flailing. We got up and we started running. Or tried to. There was panic, confusion. We ran into each other, smacking into arms, chests, elbows. We couldn't move — no escape.

There was water in my mouth, in my ears. My camera was under my shirt. Mira had vanished.

The crowd moved like a school of fish; it swayed to the right to repel a predator, then to the left to consolidate with greater strength. Right. Left. Right. Then another gust of water and the configuration broke. I was in a sea of wet fish, sweaty and angry in a swirling, hot sea.

I heard the hailer again.

Undur! Undur!

Retreat! Retreat now!

The crowd moaned. The sound was low, gurgling — now like drowning fish. The water ceased to come. Stunned bodies were exposed in their wetness. Brown. Yellow. Black. Wet eyes stared ahead at the figure on the podium. He was still there; Anwar stood strong and resolute.

'We will fight this. We will overcome this. Malaysians will rise, now! This is the time to rise!'

A tide of wet, drenched people. We could smell one another, scents unravelled, became bare, raw, ripe.

Reformasi!

Reformasi!

Reformasi!

Tens of thousands of voices, screaming in unison.

With our lungs, our hearts, our faces. Our bellies, our tongues.

Then Mira was there, by my side. She had blood on the side of her face.

What happened?

It's OK. Run. It's coming. Now!

And then we saw it. A canister flying above us, a metal bird, wingless. All eyes on it. Then another. We swirled again to avoid it, but the configuration was broken, the moment was gone. Too late. As it fell, slivers of gas escaped, streaming out like thin white fingers.

Then, it starts.

Your breath stops. Your eyes sting, like they're being gouged out with interminable ease by an interning dentist. The nerves in your nose begin to explode. Panic. Panic sets in.

I grabbed Mira.

I can't see!

I got you. Just hang on!

Run!

Lari!

Run!

To the mosque!

Shit! The gas is in the mosque!

We ran up the stairs. My slimy sneakers slipped and I crashed onto the shiny step. My eye hit the white marble floor.

My camera fell, heavy, my zoom lens thudded, then bounced with a splintering sound. Then, darkness.

My cheek was shoved into gruff carpet. I opened my eyes; my lungs heaved. I tasted gas in my mouth and I shoved my nose upwards to breathe. Above me, the cloud of gas still hung like a thin, grey shroud. Others were on the ground, retching.

Loud weeping. Strangers vomiting. A large woman in a scarf sprawled on the floor, sobbing. *Ya Allah, Ya Tuhanku, tolonglah kami.*

God help us all.

The bastards had tear-gassed the National Mosque. A sacred sanctuary.

Fucking assholes! Fuckers!

Mira hissed through a dirty towel. Her eyes were wild.

Here, breathe! It's still damp.

She took it off and gave it to me.

Take it! You're OK. You're going to get a motherfucking bruise, but you'll live.

She managed a muffled laugh.

I grabbed the towel and shoved it up my nose. Took deep breaths. It was pungent, sweaty, sharp; I almost gagged. Bile was threatening its way up my gut. I forced it back.

I looked up and saw the domed ceiling. The stark, lean curvature gave me a shiver of comfort. But the floor was covered with men and women, some prostrate, some lying down, some curled up in foetal positions. There was a dull ringing in my ears and I heard the heavy sounds of my laboured breath.

You're fine. You're safe … Mira muttered.

I nodded. Everything hurt. The insides of my head felt scorched. Fried.

Slowly we got up. Some rubbed their eyes in wonder, some still in shock. Shouts of acute pain. Splayed like spots with moving limbs.

The cloud had dissipated. The air was clear again. Air conditioning had kicked in. Vents sucked out the angry gas. Many had started praying, prostate figures. Soft murmurs surrounded me.

I pulled myself up. Shivered. Everything was still wet. My stomach churned from hunger. I turned and retched. Out came clear, yellow bile. I wanted a cold beer. A salve.

Mira nodded. She felt the same. We stumbled out, my lens still intact, and all along the street, hundreds huddled up against one another. Hugs were shared, some brave smiles. I clicked again and again, images of solidarity. Weak shouts of *Reformasi!*

I clicked the camera to autofocus and let it capture continuous frames of people stealthily disappearing into the streets.

It was dusk and the *azan* came on, blowing out of the minaret above us. A relief. The mosque still had its voice.

Allahu Akbar Allahu Akbar … A sudden music.

We grabbed each other and walked slowly, then ran, with shoes still squelching, as silently as we could into the damp twilight.

*

Two hours later, masked policemen armed with submachine guns stormed into Anwar's house in Damansara Heights and arrested him under the Internal Security Act, in plain sight of his four terrified children and his wife.

Nine days passed before he appeared in public again. He stood there before the High Court, waved his hand, and cameras from presses all over the world captured him. That image.

Our Deputy Prime Minister, right there, brutalised, beaten. His black eye was printed in every major newspaper in the world. Kuala Lumpur, city of mud, city of sin, of tear gas and riot police, would erupt again and again.

And again.

Take a city, imagine it encased in a snow globe, and shake it upside down.

Like KL. There would be no snow, of course.

But there would be zebras, tigers, giraffes, refugees, domestic workers, Bangladeshis, girls in pigtails and navy blue school uniforms, *nasi kandar* with all the condiments, chopped green chillies, beef in dark soya sauce, crab curry, cabbage with turmeric, mustard seed, and dried red chillies, guns, machetes, *parangs*, BMWs, Protons, Kancils, Ferraris, Porsches, BMW bikes, strawberry-flavoured condoms, pink ecstasy tabs, politicians, policemen, taxi drivers, footballers, red plastic chairs, dogs, cats, parakeets, rabbits, snakes, ducks, the occasional slow loris, and some of most morally reprehensible people on the planet.

We had come face to face with a reckoning, as if we had to pay for all our sins in one go and still, at the same time, find redemption. KL had unearthed a side of itself that no one had ever seen before; it was new, exhilarating, but entirely unpredictable. Thousands had woken up, but no, this wasn't like Indonesia, where Suharto had resigned. *Resigned*. He was shamed by his own people, by students who took to the streets, tens upon tens of thousands. Indonesia had witnessed three genocides, millions had died in seas of blood, but we didn't share the same script. We'd had a bloodless transition from colonial rule to independence, and just one major incident of racial rioting in 1969. But we also had an endless simmering. Of something, and everything.

But, this. This. With Anwar, we had something to fight for, something to write about.

We needed to document it, we had to write it, record it.

Fight it.

We had to fight it; we had to fight back.

And we did.

BC: This was the beginning of a larger piece of work, which I first read at the WrICE workshop in George Town. As a writer of poetry and creative nonfiction, I was unsure how to proceed with a work of longform fiction, the scale of which included the researching of actual events in Malaysian history. The manuscript, which I eventually completed at a residency in Iowa, had its first germination at our WrICE table. There, surrounded by other writers of fiction, poetry, and nonfiction, the encouragement I received was pivotal to the completion of the first draft. I knew that there was much work to be done, but key things that were said and shared with such honesty and ferocity enabled me to believe in the story I needed to tell.

THE
FAR

HIDDEN THINGS

Harriet McKnight

Carcass

The end of autumn brings afternoon storms that hang around for days afterwards. The grass is very green. In a paddock a farmer has piled old tree stumps, greyed by the weather. They are dead things. The corpse of a cow lain on top, white and tan against the grey. Legs sticking up into the air like branches.

Terra nullius

Something stalked the paddocks after dark. It had slept through the winter but the heat drew it out again. The Atkinsons lost five sheep. Their bodies were found in the mud, half-eaten.

'It wasn't any kind of beast,' they said, 'that we know of.'

This is not quiet country. It howls and churns.

My mother said I looked like the girl on the cover of *Picnic at Hanging Rock*. That's why she liked the film so much. I had that disappearing, dreamy look and that tomboy foolishness. I knew things other people didn't know. I looked good in white lace.

Miranda don't go up there come back.

A few of us went to the falls for a swim. Pale limbs on rough basalt. The kind of rock that catches soft things like ribbons and skin. We shouldn't have gone in. It's a sacred place, only for the men. Something rippled beneath stone. I covered my legs with my arms. We all began bleeding at the same time. If only we could stay out all night and watch the moon rise.

This land had swallowed girls before. Slipped them through cracks and gone. I've skinned my knees so many times they've scarred. My mother told me, watch out, the prickle of hair on your neck, the shiver that starts between your shoulder blades — you'll know it's there.

A man came from a newspaper and said the Atkinsons' sheep had markings of the extraterrestrial. The ends of the wounds too neatly sliced. On one, the jaw was removed with a surgical tool. The edges were singed and still smouldering. There was no explaining that. Animals kill by tearing and mauling. There's a hunger in the way beasts slay. But the best bits of the sheep had been left. The man took a photo for the pages, shook his head at the sky. 'We're definitely not alone,' he said. 'Evidence speaks for itself.'

He told us there was a metal disc next to the Madonna in a Yugoslavian monastery. That he'd seen the emptiness of disappeared men's mouths. They came back capable of violence. Unexplainable.

We kept an eye out for the story but it never appeared. The news cycle moved on. Two girls went missing from White Rock. They walked out of the campsite and the trees shivered. A warning. All that was left behind was a pink portable TV set.

Then the cattle got skinny, a little yellow around the eyes. They wandered the paddocks bumping into one another; their heads twitched from the neck. Some dropped right to the grass. Their bellies swelled with the rising sun. Unusually warm. All the schoolgirls were wearing black stockings. It was so warm that they removed their gloves.

You must learn to love someone else apart from me.

We lay in the paddocks and made daisy chains out of fireweed. The stems stripped our hands raw. Bradley Tyrrell said Indians use it to treat boils and cuts. The cowboy, not the curry, kind.

I had a wart on my thumb.

'We'll burn it off,' he said.

Three boys had to hold my arm flat.

It blistered for a week before it scabbed. The skin underneath was pearled and shining. The October moon waned to its thinnest edge. The oldest of the Atkinson boys cut the heads from all his chickens and made a bonfire of his clothes.

Tipping season

The Under-16s game. Like the old days, with the mud and the churned grass. The sky as rippled and tossed as the underside of the ocean surface. Electricity laced into the wind. Punches were starting to bunch up at the ends of tensed arms. Everyone's weight was shifted into their toes.

A wild boar shot out onto the grounds and everything surged forwards. Some boys from the stands jumped down and joined the players in chasing it around. The coaches screamed at them to herd it off the field. Watch the tusks, everyone was yelling.

The game was postponed. The two teams were sent to the changing rooms. Unresolved. One player shoved two balls down his shirt and walked around with enormous breasts. One stapled another's earlobe to the wall.

Rip current

My grandmother's death was like watching sand erode. For years she unravelled like a too-worn shirt. In the beginning, she didn't put on her lipstick anymore, she thought my mother was Aunty Brenda. Soon, her words dissolved from under her and she would open her mouth to find nothing on her tongue. Her hands danced to their own tune, she couldn't trust them to hold a hot pan.

My grandfather had never cooked a day in his life. He burnt the chops. The smoke alarms were too high for him to reach.

A neighbour came to see what was going on and found my grandmother chasing my grandfather around the living room.

'You rotten mongrel,' she was yelling. 'You useless man.'

We thought the fact that she'd moved so easily without help meant something.

By the time she died, she weighed forty-two kilograms. The heaviness of her coffin was in the wood.

Manufactory

You can't see where the walls were anymore but they're still there. They're what's holding the sky up. Made from bone and birthing blood. Ground down into the earth. *Our founding mothers.* Packed in with rock and heavy fists. Heels of boots pressed into their skin. Scissors held close to their scalps and snapped shut. Songs sung through stitched lips, enough to make a sailor swoon.

That's the thing about being a woman: even when you don't have anything left you still have something to sell.

First by ocean then by land, first by wood then by stone. Their wails and animal sounds were kept in. Their animal smell, their animal wants. The rippling, shuddering mass of them. Contained. They spilled their fluids over hay in the stalls like livestock. Held their offspring to their breasts amid the shit and the blood. Sewed tiny stitches into pressed cloth without leaving fingermarks, learnt manners and cooking. Rehabilitated. Dug a hole in the wall and snuck out into the smog. Leapt from the rooftops. Broke their legs on the cobblestones.

I come from a long line of women. *Founding mothers*. Twenty-five per cent have that convict blood. The thief gene passed down the female line. Mine stole her weight in stamps and then lost them. Still had something to barter, though. Unpaved streets are cold in winter. Brought in by a copper. He took a knife from his trousers, played Russian roulette with her outstretched hand. Sliced open her face for a smile. Something to wet his lips on. Pulled the cuffs on her wrists tight enough to cut skin; she was that kind of woman, she liked that.

The air was thick with lowing and the stench of a barn. *Ross Female Factory*. The exercise yard right next to the gallows. My convict mother was not alarmed. Women had been dying like this for centuries. Now by the rope instead of the flames.

Mary Wade, Joan of Arc. They all had a bit of the witch about them.

The rising sun

It was the weekend. A muggy, sticky heat by eight a.m. People carrying cases of beer, already drinking. The perfect Australian day.

Two dark boys in the middle of five thousand raised fists. A girl had her pink hijab ripped from her head. Spat on. A flag on fire in the middle of the road. A man of 'Middle Eastern appearance' in flames as well. A sea of voices: don't react. That couldn't happen in this country. You can't let them talk about us like that. Go and do something.

This is a family beach.

We grew here.

They came the way those people always come. By boats with rusted helms and sickness on board. To take things we didn't want to give. They don't understand our culture here; don't understand how hard we've worked. They throw their children into the ocean, and keep their women wrapped up.

It's not racism.

In Coogee, car windows were all smashed. The Lakemba Mosque was going to burn. A man sewed his lips together on Manus Island. Cameron Doomadgee lay still on the floor of his cell.

All the land of Egypt

We could tell the rains were coming by the flying ants. Summer afternoons ringed with purple clouds. Their fizzing wings and acrid smell.

One year, we found them in the doorjambs, under the architraves. They leaked through mortar and squeezed through glass. Our mum put out ant traps. Sat the honey in a bowl of water.

The ceiling seemed several inches lower. A writhing black surface. They flew into the windowpane. Again, again.

Red flag day

The air scalded everyone's skin long before the flames. There was no oxygen all summer. The earth split like chapped lips. Someone flicked a spark in dry grass.

This country is prone to combustion. Made of kindling and scorched twigs. Some plants need the shape of flames to bring new life. A coal seam running under sandstone on Burning Mountain has been smouldering six thousand years. But there are other fires. Ones we listen to on the radio and deliberate between staying or leaving.

Before nightfall, the winds changed. Eucalypt leaves burned their oil into fireballs. Rolled across the tops of trees. A wall of flames a hundred metres tall.

'You wouldn't believe the noise,' said a reporter. 'A warzone.'

Later, they called it an inferno. A car flew down the highway at ninety kilometres per hour with the handbrake still on and no driver. Steaks in deep freezers were cooked well-done. The roads bubbled, and sand turned to glass. In the morning, no walls, only smoke.

The ash in the middle of the fire is the softest.

First

My ancestors sailed in like driftwood, scaled masts and trees like they were possums. Crept outwards. Sea mist. Hid behind the flash and burn of gunpowder. There were bodies lined up along the riverbanks, their toes in the water.

We shove our history back down our throats. Can't say that. The wind told silent stories to the stalks of grass. A baby boy was bitten by a brown snake.

They wouldn't stop crying.

HM: Travelling to Malaysia in 2014 for the inaugural WrICE Fellowship would prove to be an exploratory journey for me, and one that was, ironically, rooted very firmly in the Australian soil I'd left behind.

Travel gave me distance to be able to view where I came from, and perspective to see how I occupied my space in the world. Buying char kway teow from the vendor across the road, drinking tequila in red-lit rooms, and walking back along sweating streets, talking and talking and talking with creative women who were certain in their heritage: none of these things would seem significant until later. My grandmother passed away when I returned, and the lineages that connected the women of my family became clearer. The cycles and echoes of those who came before me were imprinted on my own life, potent and influential in learning who I was and why I was. A great deal of the history of my country is wretched and cursed. But everywhere are stories pressed down into the earth like the sediment layers of rock. Some are only mine and others belong to all of us. This flash collection became a memoir of sorts. Something planted in another country altogether but which serves as a marker of me, here.

YOU THINK YOU KNOW

Omar Musa

I met Azmi on the bus from Kuala Lumpur to Penang. I started chatting to him because he had a brand new digital SLR camera, and since I'm a photographer and was lonely, and, well, he was sitting right next to me, it seemed like the logical thing to do. It became clear, as he spoke in his sweet, gentle voice, that he barely knew how to use the camera — in fact, it was like putting an M16 in the hands of a blind man, but we got chatting anyway. He had bad skin, the way I once did, and for some reason this problem makes me empathise with someone immediately. But there was something else beneath his deliberate gentility — a type of storminess, some secret torment.

I could understand torment. I was in Malaysia to escape a relationship gone wrong and had booked a two-week trip there on my credit card. And bought a flash new camera. Not only was my family originally from Penang, I'd heard that it was gentrification central — flaking paint and silver espresso machines. The camera loves ruin and contrast.

When we got off the bus, Azmi insisted that he walk me to my hotel. As we walked, he gave me his number and I promised that I'd give him a call. He said he worked in Komtar in a women's clothes store, nice and close.

That night I lay in the hotel room and sweated and sweated. There was a red light blinking somewhere beyond my window, and I imagined the sweat emerging in slow motion from each pore, in half-time rhythm with each blink. Maybe I was even sweating out my relationship, I thought — all the cells and thoughts and arguments that Rachel and I had shared, transmigrating from my slippery body and out into the Strait of Malacca.

I woke up feeling strangely purged and texted Azmi. He wrote back immediately and said there was a place he had to take me that served the best kueh lapis, a type of sticky, layered rice flour and tapioca cake cut into diamonds. I've never been a huge fan of it outside of how it looks, so I took more photos of the pieces than I actually ate. Azmi relished it though, daintily picking up one piece at a time and looking at it pinched between his fingers like a rare jewel.

We began to hang out every day when Azmi was on his lunch break, and he would take me to great places to eat, little holes in the wall where they made Asam laksa or Curry Mee, but never seemed to want to hang out in the evening.

He said that he lived quite far away, and became vague when pressed about it — down towards Batu Maung somewhere. I got the feeling that he didn't have that many friends and he asked me question after question about life in Australia, a torrent of questions that was almost overwhelming. But there was something incredibly sweet about the dreamy look he got in his eye, the way he said that one day he would see the Sydney Harbour Bridge. When I asked why he couldn't now, he said he had 'obligations'. He chose the word carefully and uttered it seriously.

My father used to say 'everyone has a secret in Malaysia', and I was pretty sure I knew what Azmi's was. He was gay. If you asked me how I knew, I'd say it was just because his demeanour was so camp, but maybe it was wrong of me to assume. Sometimes, I would talk about gay friends of mine, or President Obama coming out in support of marriage equality, to see how he responded. It was completely clunky and I was embarrassing myself, I know, but I wanted to give him an opening to talk freely about his sexuality. He never did. He was always polite and careful with his English, changing the subject swiftly. I could sense an annoyance increasing beneath his courteous facade, or maybe it was some kind of deep anxiety, but I in turn could not help but keep pushing.

One day, in yet another attempt to avoid the subject, he asked me if I wanted to go to the mosque with him for Friday prayers.

I was taken aback. I knew he was a devout Muslim and I thought that he could tell I was a very lapsed one indeed, especially because I would turn up hungover all the time. Maybe that was why he asked.

I hadn't prayed in years. I was surprised by how calming I found it. The ritualised, almost synchronised movement, the moment when you are sitting with your feet folded beneath you, your hands on your knees, and you point your index finger up to symbolise one god; I suddenly flashed back to praying as a child, and how I would always imagine a ray of magic light emanating from the end of the index finger, pointing out in multicoloured rays through our window that overlooked a football field and disappeared into the distant hills.

I looked sidelong at Azmi and saw that his eyes were closed tight and he was whispering intensely, private words between a man and his God.

After prayers, a man strode up to us and began to chat to us in slick English, asking where I was from and how I liked Penang. There was something authoritative and smug about the man, and I immediately disliked him. However, Azmi seemed to cower slightly, and I wondered if the man was some type of community leader or religious figure. To my dismay, Azmi invited him to lunch. The man looked at his watch and exhaled heavily before agreeing, as if he were doing us an enormous favour. It was only after ten minutes of walking to the restaurant that I realised the man was Azmi's older brother.

We sat down to lunch in a nasi kandar spot and ate with our hands. Azmi's brother talked the whole time in a way designed to be charming, meticulously collecting every grain of rice with the tips of his fingers and depositing them into his mouth. He kept checking his watch and sighing loudly, saying how busy he was, but he wouldn't stop talking about the pace of change in Malaysia, about drafting blueprints, and luncheons with Datuks.

He was clearly one of those people who like to portray their busyness as the highest of virtues. He seemed to work high up in some painful bureaucratic office job, and he was painfully proud of it. He spoke rudely to the waiters and ordered Azmi around, as if this imperiousness might impress me. Azmi was not normally this quiet.

The conversation soon turned to my love-life. I told Azmi's brother that I had been engaged to a girl called Rachel, but we had broken up and things were complicated, to put it delicately.

'Ah, yes, that's very good. You must make it work. Insya Allah, we will find Azmi a good girl to marry very soon.'

I was so astounded that I couldn't speak. Azmi was looking down, but he had clearly been through this many times before. 'Ya,'*bang*, not at the moment. I'm too busy right now. I need to get a good job first.'

Right then, I thought about secrets, about how two totally different truths can run concurrently in a mind. The brother's eyes, however, were keen and hard as he made the directive. 'No, you will not leave it too long — marriage is the most important thing. Me and your *nenek* already have somebody in mind. Insya Allah!' He then made a great show of paying for the meal and — of course, sighing heavily — said he must 'push on', the weight of the world on his shoulders. Thankfully, I never saw him again.

I went out to the streets later that afternoon, taking photos of buildings — many dilapidated, many renovated to maintain an element of ruin. Most of the shopfronts seemed to contain cool, dark interiors, and every now and then I would see some apparition in a sarong or singlet moving behind a doorway, gliding in the corner of my vision like a shadow puppet on a separate plane of existence.

Soon the heat was so oppressive that I didn't have the energy to lift the camera up to my eyes anymore. But somehow I pushed forward through the viscera of this strange, changing city. I was completely soaked with sweat but it felt wrong to stop, as if by punishing myself I might find some kind of resolution.

I finally stopped in front of a huge building, breathing hard. Its roof was caving in, and, by the looks of things, the interior had almost completely collapsed. It had once been a great hall or a rich man's house, and it looked beyond repair, as if it were somehow self-aware, ashamed that it was teetering on the edge of obsolescence. I stared deep into its guts and saw nothing but shadows, roiling ever so slowly. One swing of a wrecking ball and it would go up in a shudder of dust.

The day before I left Penang, Azmi insisted that he take me around the island. He had some friends he wanted me to meet in Batu Ferringhi. I caught a tone of admonishment when he pointed out that I hadn't left George Town anytime in this two weeks. I, too, felt guilty.

Azmi had borrowed his brother's car and we drove up the winding road, carefree, with the windows down. It took half an hour to get to the beach and the sun seemed to bobble over the water, turning it molten bronze. We ate in a Western-style café overlooking the water; the view was of a dirty sea, but the cool breeze was welcome.

When I met Azmi's friends, each one more camp than the next, I was amazed at how open he suddenly became, making loud jokes, his pockmarked face wrinkling into a big crooked grin. Everything we discussed was travel-related, their dreams of seeing the world, their frustrations that it was so expensive and that the ringgit was constantly falling. 'It is impossible to truly express who you are in this country,' one of them said. I took a photo of the five of them, with their arms around one another. Sunlight was fading fast.

As Azmi drove me back to George Town, I casually asked, 'Your friends, are they gay?' — thinking this might finally give him an opening. He looked shocked and said, 'I have no idea! We've never talked about it.' But immediately after he spoke, he put the pedal to the floor and the car began to climb in speed, faster and faster. I reached outside the window and held on out of fear. And as the car raced down the highway, which was strangely devoid of cars, we were silent, and I looked out over the darkening sea, where the only lights were far, far away.

Later that night, after he dropped me off at my hostel, I went for a long walk, letting the streets shape themselves before me. I ended up at a place that looked like a market. I suddenly smelled an intense, physical stench, and I heard a familiar sound, a kind of jostling or vibration, something I couldn't quite place. The market was empty but it didn't feel uninhabited. There were many metal surfaces for cutting and chopping and plying, and they looked wet, as if they'd been hosed down, but they were still unclean.

Then I saw the cages. Cages upon cages of chickens, with barely any room to move, some of the lucky ones able to poke their heads through the bars. They were all clucking softly to themselves in a constant rhythm, as if mesmerised by their predicament. There was one cage with six ducks in it, with a tiny bit more space. Enormous rats ran beneath the cages, so numerous that they seemed to flow into one as they moved.

I was just standing there, transfixed and staring at the scene, when I heard a whistle from across the street. It was a man sitting on his haunches, shirtless, smoking a cigarette. He beckoned me over.

I walked across the street and sat down next to him, resting my back against a street sign. His fingers were creased and scarred, and in every crease was a build-up of grease and petrol and grit.

'I watch these chickens so nobody steal them,' he said.

'You get paid for it?'

'Not much. But something.'

'It's sad,' I said.

'You no eat chicken?'

'I do.'

I lit one of my own cigarettes and we sat in silence for a minute.

'One time,' he said, 'a crazy man, a tourist from Canada, he take an axe and break the locks open on the cages. He tell the chickens and ducks to run, run free into the street. But the chickens didn't know where to go. They been in the cage too long.'

I thought about Azmi, dropping me off earlier in the night. He had wished me luck and I'd returned the sentiment. We had shaken hands, and just before I went into the hostel he said, 'You think you know. But there are many things you don't know.'

I'd looked up at him, at his smiling, serene, pineapple face, and hurriedly said, 'I know, I know,' then realised how ridiculous I sounded.

'OK,' he said, and that was it. He climbed back into the car and drove away.

I look at the photo I took of Azmi and his friends at the beach that night sometimes. I smile when I look at it, and notice the ease with which the men were resting on one another. It's not a great photo, but it's all I have of Azmi. I unsuccessfully tried to email him several times when I got back to Australia before giving up. Whenever I pick up the photo, I have to lean close to make out their joyous expressions, because their faces, mostly in darkness, turn them into ghostly cameos. Behind them, the sun swings through the dusk like a wrecking ball.

OM: I wrote 'You Think You Know' because I wanted to provide a small and subtle snapshot of the Malaysia I often visit, where there is prevalent discrimination towards LGBTI people, especially evidenced by the retention of a colonial-era penal code criminalising sodomy. I set this story against the backdrop of a rapidly changing Penang because the veneer of modernity in Malaysia makes the oppressive and regressive politics stand out even more. It is a place where conservative forces seem hell-bent on narrowing racial, religious, gender, and sexual identities. Through the narrator's brief friendship with Azmi, I wasn't aiming for an all-encompassing sociological analysis of sexual identity in Malaysia — just a keyhole into complex and deeply troubling issues. In my next novel I am hoping to plough a lot deeper, but since I didn't grow up in Malaysia and I've only started spending a lot of time there over the last five years, this vignette and a few others are a way of easing myself into writing about the nation my father comes from. I often reverse-engineer my stories from an image, as opposed to knowing the plot from the get-go. Here, the image I worked from was two men on a street corner watching chickens packed, wing to wing, in a cage.

THE DIPLOMAT'S CHILD

Robin Hemley

Nearly dawn and Jonah pads barefoot in his boxers over the freshly waxed parquet floors, to the enormous windows in the condo's living room, what his housekeeper Cherry calls the '*sala*', thirty-three floors over Manila. Fans of sunlight spread slowly over the mountains beyond Marikina in the distance.

There's no sign in the apartment of Cherry. She's been up for a while, of course — probably at the Farmers' Market in the park a couple of blocks away, buying veggies and the coffee he likes.

A large cockroach dashes past the couch and into a crack, too fast for him, and he's barefoot anyway, so he scurries into the kitchen by Cherry's room, its door cracked open.

He opens the cupboard below the sink and reaches for the Baygon spray. When he first arrived in the Philippines, he had pronounced it like an American, asking a clerk at the 7-Eleven if they had any Baygon. 'Walanang Baygon, sir,' the young woman said, pursing her lips and looking at him as though he were a little boy who'd wet his pants. 'We only have BYEgon.' She pointed to the aisle with the bug spray and then started talking in rapid Tagalog with the security guard. 'BAYgon,' the security guard repeated with an exaggerated American accent.

Jonah stalks the wall where the roach disappeared, wishing he could fog not only the roach into oblivion but the shame, both small and large shames, out of existence. It's Cherry's face that looms large in such moments, the way she regarded him last with unabashed and misplaced adoration, the way she covered her smile with her hand to hide her crooked teeth, which are not so crooked as all that, but he learned long ago that you'll never convince someone else that their imperfections are small if they believe them to be big. Natalie, whose self-criticisms were toxic, taught him that.

Last night he dreamed of a bus sailing into a gorge, the stress of this job, what he tries to shake during the day, catching up with him at night: five Americans from Florida killed a month ago when their bus to Baguio lost its brakes. The conductor survived, jumping clear before the plunge, reporting the driver had tried to hit a mango tree to stop the fall, but it hadn't worked. Not an isolated incident. Fifteen long-haul bus accidents in one year and on average ten accidents a day in metro Manila. In his dream, the bus teetered on a precipice, slipping, swaying, until the bus tipped with a sickening metallic sound, like the door of a rusty vault slowly swung open, and plummeted. He was the sole passenger on the bus. Not even a driver. When he awakened, the crankiness he felt at experiencing such a terrifying dream was amplified by his annoyance with his subconscious for concocting such an obvious metaphor for his waking emotional state. Driverless bus, indeed. Plunging into the abyss — if only he could trade in his subconscious for a more original model.

Jonah fogs the wall where the roach disappeared, the shame still fresh, and steps out of the area.

He knows he shouldn't lean on Sonora for emotional support — she's only fifteen — but he can't help himself. The call goes immediately to a message saying the caller hasn't set up her voicemail yet — though she's had the phone for over a year — so he takes a deep breath and calls Natalie instead.

'Yeah,' she answers. If sun-bleached skulls on desert floors had voices. That's the extent of the emotive power she gives him. From her, he'll never again extract even a drop of warmth. He imagines her smoking in the kitchenette, fanning the smoke in front of her. He thinks he can make out the kitchen fan thrumming in the background. She's started up again since the divorce, another reason she hates herself, another reason to inspire guilt in him. He suspects she's barely eating, either. Natalie is the kind of person so self-critical that any criticism of her by someone else is entirely counterproductive. Any blame you assign her is nothing compared to the recriminations she heaps upon herself. She knows that smoking is bad. Who doesn't? She knows that it's not good for Sonora. There's no point in saying so. 'I'll see if Sonora wants to talk,' she says. 'She just broke up with her boyfriend so she's been keeping to herself lately.'

'Boyfriend,' Jonah says as though the word isn't in his lexicon. 'Since when did she have a boyfriend?'

'Don't expect her to tell you everything. You're her father, after all.'

The unspoken words — *or did you forget?* — hover between them. Since the divorce, Natalie has not done a good job of holding her resentments in check. When she speaks of the divorce, he's learned from Sonora, she uses the word 'abandoned'.

'We're dreading this trip, Jonah. The news reports are outrageous. Every time we hear about the Philippines, it's bad news. Those poor people from Florida. How many died on that bus?'

Another thing. She speaks of Sonora and her as 'we'. As though they form one unit.

'That was … out of the ordinary,' Jonah says. 'Most tourists are completely safe unless they go looking for trouble.'

'Aren't you looking for trouble? Isn't that your nature? It seems pretty selfish to us. Will you even have time for her?' She pauses. 'I'll see if she's available.'

Like a physician's assistant announcing she'll get the doctor. Her abrupt disengagement reminds him, as if he needs a reminder, that they're nothing to each other anymore, except the parents of the person they love most.

'Hi, Dad,' Sonora says when her mother finally gives her the phone. 'Did someone die again?'

The most excruciating call he'd ever made was to the mother of a girl, the age of Sonora, who had been killed when the plane she was riding in with her father crashed on the island of Mindoro. The mother's hopeless whimpers filled the distance between them, and he had found nothing to say in the wake of her unbearable grief. Two months later he can still hear her sobs as though she had never hung up.

He made the mistake of telling Sonora about this call the last time they spoke, in response to a question about what he really did for a living. He had confessed that the memory of the woman's grief made him yearn to call Sonora immediately. A bad confession.

Sometimes, his job tires him so much that he can't even muster the energy to go drinking. His first eight months were a little less taxing, working non-immigrant visas, but for the last four months he's been working American Citizen Services (ACS), making prison visits, filing Consular Reports of Births Abroad (CRBAs), assisting in repatriation, and making death calls, constantly busy and exhausted, given that there are 350,000 Americans at any given time in the Philippines. The death calls are especially difficult, informing unsuspecting relatives that their loved ones have died in the Philippines, and arranging for the return of the remains. Working with Philippine authorities to recover bodies in remote locations.

How cold Sonora sounds now, the implied accusation that he simply needs her to lift his spirits.

'That's not why I called,' he says, though it is. Their relationship is brittle enough. The last thing she wants is to be his confessor. 'I wanted to remind you to bring a few things.'

She laughs her mother's laugh. 'I know,' she says. 'Sunscreen with an SPF of five million. Or maybe just a space suit?'

'That would get hot,' Jonah says. 'I'm just concerned. It's my job to worry.'

'That's why you're making me go there? So you can train Mom at your job? She's sure I'm going to get kidnapped the moment I set foot there.'

'You don't want to see me?' he asks.

She pauses long enough that he can feel himself starting to burst apart into fiery strands of energy, disconnected. Not that he's that fragile with anyone else, but yes, with Sonora, he's that fragile.

'Yes, I want to see you,' she says finally in a whisper, as though she doesn't want to be overheard, as though it surprises herself to hear it.

'Don't believe everything you hear about this country,' he says. 'A lot of it is beautiful. We're going to visit the island where I was born. What do you think of that?'

'This place isn't in the jungle, is it?' Sonora asks.

'Yeah, sort of. Not really.' He doesn't know. 'You *should* be interested in this trip,' he says. 'You're part Filipino, you know.' He knows he's laying it on thick, never a good strategy with a teen, and doubly so with Sonora, who has inherited her mother's deep suspicion of anyone else's enthusiasm.

'I don't even know where the Philippines are. And I don't really care. But okay, yes, I'm going. I don't have a choice, do I? What about all my other ancestors who weren't Filipino, all the Irish and Scottish and Germans? I'm just American, Dad. It's easier that way. You didn't even know Grandma.'

To think of his mother as 'Grandma' strikes him as odd — this uneducated servant girl from the provinces who had cleaned and cooked for his father, same as Cherry cooks and cleans for him. He isn't even sure if she spoke English. Probably not. His father's communication with Jonah's mother had most certainly been brief and intense, a language without words. Grandma. Jonah wouldn't even be able to speak with her. She wouldn't even know the word 'Grandma'. She had died a young woman, maybe a teenager for all he knows. Grandma.

Sonora can identify however she chooses. White mother, white grandfather, but she's not so light that she can pass. She takes after him more than her mother. She should at least know this part of her background, even if she's not ready to embrace it. He hadn't known any Fil-Ams when he was growing up in Coshocton, Ohio. All his life, people knew he was different, but unidentifiably so, and he's had to get used to other people overlaying their expectations on him. Most often, people mistake him for a Mexican-American. Even now, when he goes into a Mexican restaurant or grocery, the staff speak Spanish to him.

Sharon Robles, his high-school girlfriend, was Mexican-American, and they stood out in tiny, white Coshocton. He'd met a Fil-Am in graduate school, Nathan Portman, who passed for white and who'd mention his heritage only when he needed a cultural badge of cool. Most of the time, Nathan thought of himself as white and considered himself an observer of Filipino culture, which he found 'amusing', making Jonah so uncomfortable he rarely hung out with Nathan. Some of the

Fil-Ams he met, especially those born in the '70s, '80s, and early '90s, when the US still owned military bases in the Philippines, were the products of a predictable recipe: 1 generous helping of American military man (white works best!), viewed through rose-coloured glasses; 1 Filipina, viewed through rose-coloured glasses; shake vigorously. Important: don't remove rose-coloured glasses at this stage. Add children. Bake. Remove glasses. Let cool. Divorce bitterly, violently. Separate ingredients, refrigerate what's left of military starter. Don glasses again and repeat.

Serves two or three marriages.

Jonah wasn't like that — his father wasn't in the military but in God's army. Try to top that. The one thing he had in common with most of his friends was their lack of Tagalog, a perpetual source of frustration for many. And the blithely racist attitudes he had encountered on and off his entire life.

'Listen, I hear you broke up with your boyfriend.'

'Yeah,' Sonora says. 'It's complicated.'

On the CRBA, the Consular Report of Birth Abroad by a US Citizen, the piece of paper that had been issued to Jonah's father that made him a US citizen, the piece of paper that allowed him to move to the US with his Aunt Lonnie, this is what had been listed as the place of birth: Mabato Island. The name lives inside him — a place buried, of which he had never heard another person speak. When he was an adolescent, he found the certificate in a drawer of Aunt Lonnie's and he had visited it as if visiting his parents. He had run his fingers lightly over his parents' names, the raised seal of the United States, and tried to see through the name into the actual place — he imagined postcard scenes, palms arched over water, dolphins lolling in shallow pools, gulls circling the kind of fishing boat you might find in Alaska. What did he know about the Pacific Ocean, the South China Sea, this archipelago of seven thousand islands? He only learned enough as he grew older to modify his fantasy a little as his knowledge grew, to replace the Alaska trawlers with small catamarans, but one image remained constant: in the palm trees, he saw children sitting on the highest branches, among the coconuts; one held a machete, and he hacked away at the hard fruit until it plummeted to the sand, the shell still uncracked, but sweetness inside for those on the ground to drink.

'Yeah,' he tells his daughter. 'It's almost always complicated.'

RH: This piece is an excerpt from my recently completed novel, *The Diplomat's Child*. The novel is set in the Philippines today as well as twenty-five years in the future, and is very much about a search for lost fathers and ultimately a father–daughter story. Jonah Fletcher is a low-level bureaucrat at the US embassy in Manila, responsible for notifying the relatives of Americans who die there, making prison visits, and arranging emergency loans. When he decides to take his estranged teenage daughter to the pristine island of his birth, Jonah is hoping for a much-needed holiday that might give their strained relationship a new start, but he soon learns that in a small country there's no escaping the past. Haunted by the sins of his father, and helpless in his attempts to reconnect with his daughter, Jonah's bumbling missteps land him right where he started: unwittingly ensnared in the politics of an 'undiscovered' paradise. In the course of the novel, we see Jonah's daughter Sonora as a fifteen-year-old visiting her divorced dad as well as twenty-five years later, as a freshman Congresswoman from Massachusetts, in turn presented with the mystery of her father's life and the secrets he kept from her. The Philippines is a country I love, and I've married into the culture. I speak a fair bit of Tagalog, know the history and much of the literature, and have spent years of my life there. Like just about everyone I know, I'm fascinated by issues of identity, especially where notions of identity are fluid, even unstable, in the face of self-doubts, self-deceptions, and the mythologies of our parents.

A LETTER IN THREE PARTS OR MORE

Melody Paloma

1

Tugboat moored by the air-conditioning unit
until we pressed an erumpent hill of old blood
which becomes my throat/is also a test tube of honey.

We've often found things to say about bodies
not necessarily ours —
but this time his hand was pretty steady
and the ultrasound screen was a lot like yours
with little fish, which we've found again is only blood
                              no less interesting.

And it did look old, at least not swimming
nothing worth coddling
although worry rarely works like that.

This dashboard begs for shoplifting
all its pieces shifting, well-liquored
dentist's chair
operating table
ultrasound machine
rubbing in the warehouse
the clinical come foul —
well-preserved and susceptible to rust.

2

never ever etc.
at least not like that
only in the way that you might
adopt my reading posture in pyjamas
like how a skull is also a jewellery box

only in the way
we wear swans on our heads
in hotel rooms
and contemplate the gift economy
of bananas

only in the way that same ant
keeps coming back
or we allow oil to heat
(just enough) before it spits

only in the way
my dead focus keeps a splinter
in escalator pinch

only in the way I
borrow little diddies
for the knick-knackatorium

and only in the way that there's the potential
to try this new thing
where I like Justin Bieber

as wild as lying horizontal
across the bed.

3

There's not much that stays still under skin,
a strange thing to Google
I suppose that's why this time it's
                              worth removing.

All our best shimmying happens
with wide air for speaking
—— real conversation only
in our scratching of ankles.

How would we cope if we moved a little faster?
Already you run ten kilometres a day
and I twitch as much as possible
in my sleep.

In clichés I tend to hold your hand on planes
level myself halcyon to
compensate your shaking.

Basically, we should catch this fever at the same time
but better to keep the dreams to yourself

and otherwise, in separate bedrooms rearranged
I'll feel us both seize up, orchestrally.
How about in cars? How we accept the need for quiet
the analysis of hum.

Again elsewhere and on bicycles
you tell me you remember all our houses
through the kitchen window
hands floating and
detached.

MP: For me, writing poetry is a correspondence, a conversation with
people, places, things, and texts. WrICE activated this understanding,
revealing the ways in which writing and reading operate in a constant
mode of production, as an infinite assemblage of thoughts and ideas.

As a writer, I aim to obscure and challenge the inherent modes of consciousness that exist around language. As a reader, following the offshoots and peripheral ideas that come with varying relationships to language and revelling in the ways these can be simultaneously embraced and obscured is, for me, both brilliant and thrilling. So I try to pay attention to the way in which we share language — its shifts, and how it creates meaning. These poems exist as a part of an exchange between myself and WrICE fellow Amarlie Foster, as a nod to the importance of creative exchange between writers and as thanks to WrICE for embracing the development of relationships and ideas.

INCOMING TIDES

Cate Kennedy

The tour guide's business card, presented to me like the ace of spades, promises comfort and reliability, hundreds of satisfied customers, and a customised adventure. Also, he's a 'funny guide' who speaks English well. But at eight o'clock the next morning it's not the funny guide who shows up with a motorbike and two helmets: it's his associate, who, alas, does not speak English at all.

Funny guide's been called away, clearly, on a bigger and more lucrative tour, so I am able to explore the villages and back roads around Hoi An on the back of a motorbike unencumbered by explanation or spiel, free to think my own thoughts, and content, for a morning, to be having a break from the intensive workshopping of the WrICE residency.

We putter through a maze of little communities, the noisiest thing in a tranquil landscape. These old narrow tracks and pathways have been worn smooth by feet and pushbikes, and as we pass old people and dogs, both sitting on front porches, somnolent in the morning sun, they look up at the sound of the approaching motorbike to see if they recognise us. All around the villages stretch rice paddies, and around the houses are neat gardens of lettuce and greens in well-tended rows, flat baskets of silver fish laid out to dry, and vegetables sliced ready for pickling. I glimpse inside these houses, with their tidy tables and chairs and neat stacks of cooking pots; the atmosphere one of overriding unhurried order.

Of course a closer look shows the industry under the tranquility — women planting rice, men harvesting rice, people watering, digging, and preparing vegetables to load into baskets to ride to market. I fall into a sort of dreamy somnolence myself, gazing at these plots of flowers and vegetables, the chickens, buffaloes, dogs, and roosters, the workers building new houses and patios, and the pragmatic aspiration shown in the ubiquitous bouquets of reinforcing rods sprouting into the air from single-storey constructions, ready for the second level someday.

'Cua Dai beach?' says my reticent guide when we stop and take off our helmets. He's got a booklet of brochures and postcards of tourist spots within motorbiking distance, and he points to one showing a golden beach fringed with palm trees.

'Sure,' I say, and we head out of the rice paddies and onto the sealed road leading away from Hoi An.

Cua Dai beach is big — almost three kilometres long and in places three hundred metres wide, and in fact the beach keeps going thirty kilometres all the way to Da Nang city, but its famed pristine sands and palm trees, its lining of posh resorts and rustic seafood restaurants and sparkling water, its full moon, grilled lobster, and candlelit glamour — all come to an abrupt precipice at the southernmost end. Something odd is happening to the beach here — it's disappearing. It's as if the sea has changed its mind, and wants all that sand back, thanks very much.

Cua Dai literally means 'Big Sea Mouth', and here it is literally sucking and gnawing, eating the beach away like a big slice of melon. Trucks pull up to deposit loads of fresh sand from elsewhere, and teams of men labour to fill giant sandbags to bolster what's left in place, while forklifts and graders, like toys in a giant sandpit, wheel around reshaping piles and contours.

There are rows of replanted palm trees and a long, incongruous, rust-red steel wall built in the water, corroded with salt, trying in vain to hold back the incoming tide. The sea slops and slurps and gurgles through the cracks with each wave. The beachside resorts unfortunate enough to find themselves alongside the line of erosion are clearly feeling the dissonance between the brochure and the reality.

The sand plunges steeply down to the water at an incline you wouldn't want to be negotiating at night with a cocktail in one hand and your shoes romantically dangling from the other. There are layers of sandbags in front of the restaurants battened down in place with wire armature, with more sand over the top raked to give the illusion of solidity. The machinery stands starkly against this building-site landscape as workers toil away with rakes, literally rearranging the deckchairs as I watch.

The sea is not blue and turquoise and limpidly clear as in the TripAdvisor photos: it is rough and it is coming in. A few intrepid souls are out braving its currents, and in the hazy distance local fishermen in their basket boats sit fishing beneath parasols.

I've been keen to check out some of these famous bamboo basket boats firsthand, and not just the mainland ones that have been converted into lounge chairs, so it's great to see a pair of them heading out into the breakers, the fishermen inside using their oars to slide the flexible boats cleverly over the surf and out into the open water. It might seem flimsy and precarious, taking to the ocean in a large waterproofed basket, but the fishermen on this coast seem completely relaxed and at ease in their graceful bamboo craft.

A few days later we're dodging incoming waves of an entirely different nature — a veritable tsunami of motorbikes in the chaotic Old Quarter streets of Hanoi. They are ten deep and never-ending. They ignore traffic lights and boundaries, simply driving up onto the footpath and swirling through if there's a hold-up somewhere in front of them. They roar through intersections in all directions, their riders sometimes in helmets and sometimes not, but usually in face masks or scarves against the pollution and grit.

Sometimes the motorbikes are carrying four or five people, sometimes twenty cages full of chickens, sometimes enormous towering strapped-together constructions of delivery boxes. I see feather dusters, toilet paper, artificial flowers, precarious towers stacked a storey above and around their fearless riders. I note all this because I am frozen, gobsmacked on the teeming pavement, too intimidated to cross the road, waiting like the small-town hick that I am for a break to scurry through.

It doesn't happen. The motorbikes just keep coming, millions of them, ducking and weaving on the roaring tide, giving other riders and vehicles the narrowest berth imaginable. They skirt and swerve around the astonishing mirage of a small, wiry old lady in a conical hat determinedly trudging through the same intersection holding suspended bamboo poles with fruit and vegetables in two baskets, making her inexorable way from A to B.

They put me to shame, these resolute old ladies. They're made of way sterner stuff than me. And then there are the young girls on pushbikes pedalling through the mayhem, elegant and seemingly quite relaxed. I'm only standing on the street corner and I'm already a gibbering wreck; the thought of wading into the maelstrom on a pushbike is inconceivable. Not these girls. I'm sure if I stood here long enough I'd see one singing casually along to a song on her iPod. Possibly even texting, with her phone resting on the handlebars. Just a generation ago everyone rode pushbikes here — back in 1979, the population of the city was one million; now it's seven times that much. And they all have motorbikes, take it from me.

There's just so much of everything, and everything is knitted in to the hive of industry on its way from production to consumption. The corner snack bar with the plastic tables outside, bordered with painted line beyond which motorbikes, in theory, should not travel, seems to sell only pumpkin seeds. The clusters of plastic stools are thronged with young people eating pumpkin seeds, their mouths working on them and their conversation, with each other and on the phone, while around their feet, in drifting eddies like ocean debris, lie piles of discarded pumpkin-seed husks.

How to negotiate this roaring traffic, unstoppable as a tide pouring through what was once, you can see, a stately boulevard but is now an artery of iron and fuel and propulsion? There is no way, say the locals firmly, except to simply step out into it. Don't look left or right, or you will lose your nerve.

And whatever you do, don't stop. If you hesitate in your desperate forward wading, someone will hit you. They don't want to hit you any more than you want to be hit, but they're doing complex physics in their heads as they ride, figuring out whatever it is — speed times velocity times trajectory, or something — and you hesitating or attempting to tentatively dodge the tide will mess up their calculation of your own vector.

You must fix your eyes upon the far shore, or perhaps just shut your eyes completely, and walk straight out into ten lanes of traffic. It's the only way. So the current of motorbikes and buses and the occasional veering taxi is intersected, periodically, by little knots of grim pedestrians doing the same suicidal, determined dash.

*

The word for 'motorbike' in Vietnamese is *xe om*, which, fittingly, is pronounced *'say om'* — exactly what you need to do as you take a deep steadying breath before stepping off the kerb.

Figuratively speaking, *xe om* also means 'hug the driver' — another thing I'd be doing if I were ever forced to get on the back of a motorbike in Hanoi. My hug would be a death grip, I'm sure.

Mostly, though, I am occupied just managing my own two feet. Sometimes a perfect storm occurs, where industry, trade, and breakneck development seizes the artery like a blood clot, immediately banking up a boiling mass of activity in all directions. Complications include a street-front display bursting from a shop door, a jam-packed row of parked motorbikes, a stream of couriers carrying towers of Chinese New Year decorations, and an oncoming bus. At ground zero of this clot will be, let's say, a cauldron of boiling oil on the footpath, surrounded by people hunching their plastic seats closer to eat fried dumplings as tourists stop to admire the storefront display as motorbikes mount the pavement to avoid the jam ahead as the solidly packed row of parked motorbikes creates a solid wall impossible to traverse by foot, pushbike, vendor cart, taxi, or wheeled trolley. Amid the honking, blaring, shouting, and gesturing, jackhammers will be going about their business, endlessly hacking up old concrete to make way for new, exposing pipes in the gutter, water flowing and pooling, the gas bottle heating the boiling oil vibrating and teetering. And all of it threatening, to my bumpkin eyes, to go arse-up in the most cataclysmic way imaginable, every moment.

And yet the motorbikes slow to a revving throb, feet hit the road to balance the twenty cages of chooks or watches or fabric or dry-cleaned suits or whatever the hell they've strapped on there, a couple of plastic chairs are scraped an inch this way, the cement mixer idles an inch back that way, everyone waits for the clot to clear somehow, and then the great heart pumps again and it swirls on; deafening, relentless, infinitely collective.

The trick is not to stand still, not to be in the way. Be purposeful. Grab your chair, grab your bowl of soup, watch your toes, don't lean on that stack of motorbikes propped on the kerb, and just hold tight. Say 'om'. Commerce is exploding around you in a shimmering haze on every level imaginable, from the glass and steel buildings of the country's burgeoning nouveau riche to the men who hang around the front doors of the tourist hotels, offering to fix your shoes with a thirty-cent tube of superglue they're brandishing.

The onslaught assaults the senses, overwhelming the fading grandeur of the Old Quarter. But like most organic systems, it's not chaos; it's ardent, individual aspirational endeavour wrapped in a collective work ethic that's astonishing. It's a determined drive, and I can feel the other writers on my Fellowship program choosing their words with increasing care as they speak to the student guides accompanying us with such beaming diligence, and to the television crews in Hanoi, eagerly interviewing each one of us about our impressions of Vietnam.

It's not crazy busy, it's … vibrant! It's not overwhelmingly noisy, frenetic, and anarchic, it's … developing and dynamic! When some of the millions of people who ride motorbikes in

Hanoi decide their next upwardly mobile goal is a car, those streets are going to be … completely gridlocked! We don't say this, of course, because who knows what the Vietnamese Ministry of Transport will come up with before then, to make these wide elegant streets and boulevards actually strollable again, not to mention visible?

Then again, maybe it's just me finding the metropolis too overwhelming to take in. I've done a bit of research on the website Vietnam Online, and fascinating as the city is, I'm having a hard time reconciling what I'm looking at with the upbeat descriptive reportage. This part of the city, says the article, is not only the oldest but the busiest and most interesting. *'Every street is winding, intimate, and shady'*, it claims. *'At night the lights of storefronts keep the streets lit and animated … In the Ancient Quarter the most appealing mode of transportation for those who do not care to enjoy the "36 Streets" on foot is the cyclo.'*

We visit the Temple of Literature, established in the tenth century and functioning as a university for the country's royalty and elite from 1076 to 1770, which is a pretty amazing record. *('You can not help being overwhelmed by the serenity of Van Mieu (Temple of Literature) and Quoc Tu Giam (National University) from the moment you pass through its towering gates. Together, they make one of Asia's loveliest spots.')*

On display there, just beyond the Constellation of Literature pavilion and the Well of Heavenly Clarity, are statues and stelae of the Temple's famous doctors through the centuries.

The carved, headstone-like stelae, of which about eighty remain, give the names and birthplaces of 1,307 graduates of the royal exams held between the fifteenth and the eighteenth centuries. I know this because our charming student guides translated for me, when I was intrigued to know why so many of them appeared to have been attacked with chisels and their ancient Chinese engravings erased. What had been carved on these slabs of stone? Memorable or particularly pithy aphorisms of famous sages? Quotable quotes from the academic year?

The students are unsure. The characters on the stelae praise the dynastic monarch of the time and, you'd have to presume, add some immortal bit of advice or wisdom about studying literature in the first place. So why the defacements? Perhaps subsequent scholars and professors didn't like or approve of their sentiments, suggest the students. Maybe they, in turn, then ran the risk of having their own zingers ignominiously erased, or maybe it was a dynastic decree.

In any case, history has a way of being built over and erased, pressed beneath layers of the new. Most of the Vietnamese population now are too young to remember the conflict we know as the Vietnam War but which they call the American War. You'd have to look very hard to find signs that enemy forces ever bombed Hanoi; the determination to chisel smooth the scars of the past, rebuild, repair, and move on is palpable.

The ubiquitous public address system still blares morning news bulletins into the streets in a faintly Orwellian reminder of the Communist regime, but along with the other remnant paraphernalia — the Vietnamese flags, Ho Chi Minh T-shirts, and billboard propaganda converted into fridge magnets and badges and cigarette lighters — Communist party ideology, at least at the pumping street level, seems weirdly distant and anachronistic, almost irrelevant, almost a tongue-in-cheek bit of retro chic.

Walking crabwise through these streets, trying to find a way to avoid crossing a road, I see thriving micro-enterprise everywhere — traditional lacquerwear, pho stalls, silk tailors, tea, jewellery, paintings, French pastry shops, Chinese medicines, bootleg DVDs, iPhone covers, and streets full of red, gold, and white decorations and artificial flowers ready for religious ceremonies. There's so much of it that my eye stops registering the details, and starts looking for more startling examples of kitsch and memorabilia.

At Hoa Lo Prison, walking shell-shocked past the guillotine and torture dioramas in this deeply unhappy building, I pass through the souvenir shop and find, tumbled in with the postcards and guidebooks, some colourful packages of antique and discontinued Vietnamese and French-issued stamps in silk-covered albums, exactly like the one my father brought home for me in 1974. It gives me a stab of recognition, nostalgia, and grief, remembering these albums, and the exotic Vietnamese dolls and lacquer music boxes that he sent home to me and my sister that dreadful long year when he was posted to Vung Tau. The Vietnam War. The American War. The presents came wrapped in Vietnamese newspapers, covered in indecipherable text that as an eight-year-old I looked at wonderingly, astonished that something so incomprehensibly strange could exist in the world and be read and understood by a whole country of people I would never meet. Standing here, I realise I still have no shared language even now, over forty years later, much as I would like to have a conversation with the shop owner about these souvenirs.

There were two other moments on this residency I wished more than anything I could speak Vietnamese — both involving a moment of stillness and serenity when I felt most acutely the yearning for a quiet conversation, rather than the reflex of groping for my phone to record the moment.

The first was seeing an elderly man in the Reunification Palace in Ho Chi Minh City, seated cross-legged, head bowed, in front of the roped-off display of the war command room. As the daughter of a veteran, scenes from this palace's history were burned into my memory: watching, as a child, TV footage of the victorious North Vietnamese Army's assault through the palace gates in 1975, images of panicked people scrambling from the roof of the US embassy, clawing and fighting their way into helicopters to escape. My dad has passed away now, but his presence was very much at my shoulder as I stopped, filled with sadness, and watched this humble, straight-backed old man sitting on the floor before the display room, meditating quietly and with such dignity. I wished I knew whether he called this city Ho Chi Minh or

Saigon, what he was thinking, who he had lost, how he had survived. He looked as tough as nails, thin and sinewy as a vine.

The other moment was coming back over the bridge into Hoi An on the rear of my silent guide's motorbike, when we happened upon what years ago you would have called a Kodak moment. Amid the bustling new development, with its industrious jackhammering, the piles of rock and masonry and the surging traffic roaring in and out of the town, another old man was sitting quietly, fishing on the still and tranquil river in a picturesque little sampan, thinking his own thoughts. Again, I would have given a lot to know what they were.

In a passing blue and green watercolour moment, which would have captured old Vietnam's quintessential calm, the brightest dot of jarring incongruity came from him. He was wearing a fluorescent safety vest, and I don't blame him.

CK: Travelling to a different culture and taking part in a writing program with people from a range of countries and with a diverse mix of lives and languages was a fascinating and intense experience, and one which — inevitably maybe — brought with it many thoughts about silences, miscommunications, and untold stories. The most deeply felt experiences are just straight-out hard to communicate, even in your own language. The bond I grew to feel with the other writers, though, eventually seemed to transcend difficulties with language. We read one another our stories (even when English must have felt like a blunt instrument), listened and tried to respond in the spirit of sharing, shed a few tears of recognition, and then hit the streets to take in another dose of amazing Vietnam. On our last night together there were a few speeches, jokes, and songs. I remember Melody saying of the residency: 'It's made me realise that this is what I want to do.' She meant the idea of being a writer, no doubt, but there is so much more in that statement. You're by and large alone with your own ideas when you write, wandering around in isolation like a stranger in a strange land. It's the possibility of connection and recognition that keeps you going, hoping to see a familiar face across the medium of the page, and realising there's a more universal language and understanding that you share, despite everything that makes you different.

BG: THE SIGNIFICANT YEARS

Xu Xi

Before Google (hereinafter BG), there was no failure of the open page. The year, of course, was 2004, 19 August specifically — two days after Indonesia celebrated independence from the Dutch is my mnemonic, given my former nationality.

That day was the birth of GOOG, the company's stock ticker symbol. Post-Google (hereinafter PG) began that day, to wit, 1 PG. The calendar thereafter was easy to establish, despite the leap year, thanks to Microsoft Excel, and 1 BG was now the date formerly known as 18 August 2004.

It should be noted that some historians argue the PG calendar really began in January 1996, when Larry Page was rooting around for a dissertation project. In fact, the TruGoogol[1] Group still maintains an oppositional calendar (PG — Prior to Google — and OG — Once We Were Google), but its inelegant nomenclature, as well as failure to identify a specific date, doomed it from the start. TruGoogol will likely be silenced in time, along with the other diehards of the true millennium.

The Chinese have a similar calendar, or rather the Republic of China does. These days we might say the 'former' republic, as there is only 'one China' according to China, and even according to the US, which is at least consistent about this one, although allegiances have shifted over time. The superpowers of any moment are the ones that count, in the moment that is, despite democracy and vox populi, since Taiwan is still 'Formosa' to some and 'the Chinese Republic' to others.

So 1912 is Chinese year one, if you track time from the founding of a republic and the end of dynastic rule. Google was, after all, formerly 'googol', which, unlike its successor, did not achieve Proper Nounhood, but that is another history. But if you google[2] the Chinese calendar, it becomes instantly apparent that in the history of calendars, we still have no idea where in time we really are, since a little whimsy, and the moment, dictates our notion of how to count, how to measure, how to perpetuate time, although in the PG era you own all time in the form of the perpetual calendar. If I care at all about the Chinese alternative it is only because of my former right to Chinese citizenship, as one who belongs to that peculiar minority, the 'overseas Chinese' or *wah kiu*[3] — a right now revoked, although I do have the right of permanent abode in a tiny corner over which China has sovereignty, the SAR,[4] or formerly, Hong Kong.

Which brings me, finally, to the significant years.

BG 43 (circa AD 1961 to '62)

I discovered world citizenship: not, as Wikipedia suggests, the philosophical or altruistic ideal, but the real deal, one with a passport. It was something I read in one of the four Hong Kong English newspapers of the day (all but one now virtually obsolete), and being a bored teen, wrote away immediately for further information.

Perhaps a fortnight later (it's difficult to recall correctly the feeling of time BG), an airmail packet appeared in my family's mailbox. The papers, those mysterious, official documents, explained in plain language how I could obtain this passport that would allow me to travel freely worldwide. I need belong to no nation and could speak what language I chose. There was, however, a caveat. This travel document was only recognised by a few nations — fewer, I noted, than even those who did not require visas of my Indonesian passport. Those papers are lost now, a matter of some regret, but space was at a premium in tiny Hong Kong and other printed matter engaged me instead once I got over my adolescent disappointment.

It was Garry Davis who, sometime between 60 and 59 BG, renounced his US citizenship in Paris and founded a World Government, the organisation that later issued the passport I sought. At the age of twenty-six, this bomber pilot pursued a belief that nations and borders unnecessarily divided us. 'I feel impelled to express to the young war veteran Davis my recognition', said Albert Einstein, 'of the sacrifice he has made for the general welfare of mankind ... he has made of himself a "displaced person" in order to fight for the natural rights of those who are the mute witnesses of the low moral level of our time.' Over the years, such luminaries as Yehudi Menuhin expressed support for him and his cause. In approximately BG 17, Richard Falk at the Center of International Studies, upon receiving Davis's materials, responded that he shared 'the basic impulses that motivate your activity. It is ahead of its time, but embodies an outlook that needs to become accepted if our species is to endure and survive'. Google has been kind to Davis. As recently as BG 2, Davis's website still promoted his cause.

BG 35 (circa the academic year 1970 to '71)

The Institute of International Education (hereinafter IIE) on Hong Kong island had a library. There were large volumes there, larger even than the *Encyclopedia Britannica* at home, that listed colleges and universities in America and the courses of study available. I knew about SATs, and had already applied to take them. But to which university across the Pacific to apply was something I knew nothing about.

My mother was frantic about our financial state (*destitute!*, which we were not, but melodrama was her strong suit) and my father was depressed, as he had been since his business failed some five years earlier. Informed judgement was not their strong suit. My grades were nothing like those of my smart cousins who could apply for and get academic scholarships, even at the Ivies. There would be no scholarships for me and even though I didn't know much, I knew enough to know that foreign students were expected to foot their own bill.

I was also the eldest child, that tedious experiment, who must blaze trails without compass, map, or even the right baggage or footwear. Meanwhile, my parents argued about money, about life, about what education girls really needed, about how impossible it was to afford university abroad.

Before I discovered the IIE, I scoured want ads for jobs that required only a secondary education, and applied for and got a position in insurance sales. Upon presenting this accomplishment to my parents, there was a stunned absence of argument. *No*, they both said, *you will go to university abroad*. Now that my future course was clear, all I had to do was find a university, something about which my parents remained surprisingly silent.

The first thing my research revealed was that all schools offered English as a degree. This was startling to me. Google had not yet opened the door to this kind of knowledge; it remained daunting across borders. It soon became apparent that I could read these reference volumes for years and still have no idea why one university was better than another. The concept of a university tour was more than foreign — it was unimaginable when even my plane fare would be hard to find. In retrospect, I might have done better at insurance sales, much like Wallace Stevens did, although having not read much American literature, thanks to a stunted British colonial education, Stevens was still a future book for my shelf.

My IIE research yielded an initial longlist of schools. I wrote to them, and rejected any that addressed their reply to

'Hong Kong, Japan', because even though I didn't know much, I wanted my university to know more than me, not less. In the absence of informed judgement, there is merely decision, and I did decide in favour of, one, a Catholic education, since mine was reasonably good and somewhat American under the Maryknoll order, and, two, a place to which I wished to go. Which translated to Xavier in Ohio and the University of Minnesota, the first being obvious and the second because Mary Tyler Moore, or rather her TV persona, was situated in Minneapolis. I applied to and was accepted at both. Of course, had I been a student in the PG era, there's no telling where I might have ended up. The University of Colorado, no doubt, because South Park is in that state.

Some years later, around BG 25, I did again open a book, to practice for the GREs, an exam that was rather difficult to arrange for because I was in Greece and of no fixed abode. I sat it in a suburb of Paris, which is daunting in retrospect because I cannot for the life of me imagine how I found the information, how I arranged payment without a credit card, how the Greek postal system did not fail me given my lack of knowledge of Greek.

Time must have been more elastic then, because it seems I could wait and plan, well ahead of the moment of execution, to write away for knowledge, to haunt libraries and various information centres long before the internet café was a fixture on city corners, in laundromats and bars. All I can swear to is that by BG 25, my judgement was better informed because I ended up in Amherst, Massachusetts, Emily Dickinson's home, which seemed as good a reason as any to be in a place.

BG 27 (during my terrible twenties)

Telex had entered my life, along with the electric typewriter, one that had two font balls and even memory in the form of cartridges, an astounding technology. It was also a profound moment to be working for the airlines, especially in Asia, where the economies were not yet tigers and the Thai baht had not crashed and precipitated an economic crisis. Data could be processed by nerds on the mainframe, and my mission, not impossibly, was to collect this data and turn out a frequent flyer program, a grand new marketing thing that would put our company on the map. There was a typing pool and plenty of paper, even carbon paper for file copies. Burnt offerings now, I imagine, like the paper cars, homes, computers, cell phones that Chinese people burn for their dead today. Carbon copies, up in smoke, sacrificial lambs to the gods of small and smaller bytes.

But telex was grand. As an 'officer' grade in the company, I had my own airline telex address. All I needed was the corresponding address to any other airline personnel in the world, and I could write a message, hand it to the operator, and within a day or two, someone on the other side of the world could read a printout of my message in her or his inbox. Excellent for official communication, but even better for unofficial ones, like the messages I sent to the guy I was dating at Braniff, based in Honolulu. We created code, the standard being his reservations request for bookings at the Broadcast Hotel, a fictional locale, the name of the street where I lived. It was how he said he was coming to town.

By the late BG era, there were multiple email options, instant messaging, and by the time PG came to pass, even twittering on devices that marry phones and laptops. With all those myriad ways, means, addresses, how does anyone find you anymore?

BG 20 (during the dog days of summer)

At the Cincinnati Public Library, the Census was a matter of record. I sat in the library for hours, trying to comprehend the mass of reports about America's population. Specifically, I needed data on ethnic groupings, because I had a research contract with a diversity consultant who did cross-cultural sensitivity training and wrote case studies for corporations about minority hires.

In that same library, I was later to pore over volumes of business directories, identifying likely companies who would hire me. In a bid to move to New York City, I wrote two hundred letters on a box called an Apple, one that resembled a portable television, using a program called MacWrite, and watched the pages rattle out on my brand new dot matrix printer. It was a little tricky, aligning those holes to catch correctly on the print roll, but significantly faster than my old electric typewriter, which lasted about as long as eight-track tapes. I had my 3" x 5" disk with the master letter that could be overwritten two hundred times. If I really wanted to, I could have saved all two hundred letters, but that would have taken up too much disk space, since memory en masse was still future shock. The purchase of this ancient set-up required an abiding faith in my ability to pay off credit-card debt.

Re-reading the previous paragraph, I realise I ought to consider footnotes, especially for the idea of paying off debt. Such references might ultimately lose their original meaning in our PG era, if they are not already considered archaic, which only confirms my suspicion that time has changed, is changing even as I breathe.

But the Census, fortunately, is still understandable. After weeks of research, I was able to compile a summary of the Asian population in America, which was my task. Asians comprised 1.97%, a shockingly low number, and that included Native American, Inuit, Eskimo, and Middle Easterners. Still a green card alien then, I began to see my identity in a new light. Previously, as a foreign student, I had considered myself part of a worldwide populace of multiple ethnicities, some mixed-race like myself. For the first time as an almost-American, I understood the meaning of 'minority'.

By the PG era, the Census felt more user-friendly because Asians had risen to just shy of 4%, exclusive of Middle Easterners this time, and some say the number could rise to as high as 10% by the time PG 42 rolls round.

BG 18 (as autumn leaves drifted by my window)

I pledged allegiance, to a flag, I mean. Fortunately this was a choral endeavour, because I stumbled over the indivisibility of one nation. It was a time of great divide because some sizeable percentage of the nation's wealth was held by a tiny percentage of the populace. The stock market crashed, the economy tanked, and I was laid off from my job thanks to a merger and acquisition, Wall Street's grandest Ponzi, one in which I was not quite senior enough to benefit from the golden handshake, this job that had brought me to New York, the one that two hundred letters and three rounds of interviews had finally yielded, interview rounds paid for by excessive corporate exuberance that flew and housed and wined and dined me in Kansas City and New York. Don't ask, don't tell was the name of the game.

But I did have my blue US passport now (even though I couldn't afford to travel), and the right to vote (which, fortunately, was free), and even the right to sit in judgement of those who did not view the law as an abiding concern. What more could you want in Life BG? So I trudged along to the office of unemployment and took my place in line with my fellow Americans.

It was a profound experience. For once I wasn't a minority because the minority was the majority in that government office, doing the hustle towards redemption. One step forward, two steps back, side step, back step, side step, back step. Again and again and again. My fellow Americans were kind enough to teach me the dance and to them I am grateful, those anonymous citizens who were much less likely than I to be entrepreneurial, to quickly find freelance work, to send out résumés each day from a transition office my company provided, to network and interview with sympathetic souls, to learn the latest technologies of LANs and WANs and desktop publishing, an arcane term now but one that ensured my next full-time position in a Wall Street law firm some eighteen months later.

They, unlike me, did not have former colleagues to take them to lunch or offer moral support, did not have books to turn to for solace, did not have degrees and keys and rooms of their own to shelter them in troubled times. Yet they taught me the dance, that joyless hustle, because I too was one of them, in line, battling the same bureaucracy in order to pay the rent, to eat, to hold me over until the next taxable salary cheque. There are no minorities in a country that values the rights of all citizens, whoever they are, whatever their circumstances and means. Of all the offices of the government of the United States I was to visit that year, this was the most significant.

The years to follow as the BG era approached its end tested the nation's indivisibility. The borders between 'to have' and 'to hold' widened, became a chasm of national impossibility as debt mounted and irrational exuberance took hold, as the World Wide Web spun and spanned divides, but on threads so tenuous they broke whenever we sighed.

Shall I leap or shall I stay? Or place hope in my next life as real life crashes so painfully down, thanks to bombs and planes and the loss of faith in holding hands across humanity? Meanwhile the zealots' faith is reason to fight, reason to hate, reason to close down the borderless world of the web except to hackers and malcontents.

A failure of the open page. A blank.

And here the system crashed, as systems must in the BG world of planned obsolescence, destroying all records except these. In our PG era now, we recall the BG time with both affection and distaste, wishing for a less perpetual calendar in the history of the world, whether BG, AD, BC, CE, BCE, or before and after the founding of the first Chinese Republic.

And I am merely a chronicler of fictions, histories, calendars, believing that this era too must be recorded, somehow, even if paper will go up in flames, even if the disappearance of carbon copies transforms the language of acronyms, even if memory is cheap, selling itself to the highest bidder like love for sale, even if what is remembered is selective, even if there is no way of knowing what the years ahead will bring except for the perpetual motion of calendars and time. Time feels different now. Already PG begins to feel old and the blank page adopts a new identity. The server unexpectedly drops connections, which sometimes occurs when servers are busy, but take heart, dear one, you may be able to open the page later, and later means the calendar, the era continues, that time has not ended yet.

At least the significant years survive.

---

1   TruGoogol is an invention. This is a liberty of 'creative' nonfiction.
2   The verb, distinguished by lowercase status.
3   Also, *hua qiao* in Putonghua or Mandarin, a one-time political designation for Chinese overseas, particularly those of us in South-East Asia. The ones patriotic enough to heed the call of 'loving the nation' were led to far-flung corners of said nation during the Cultural Revolution, resulting in the loss of any citizenship, as happened to some members of my family. *Wah kiu* is Cantonese and the term no longer carries its former political weight.
4   Special Administrative Region — although why a city on a bunch of mostly uninhabited islands should be a 'region' is anybody's guess.

XX: The problem in writing memoir is always my instinct for privacy, which is why I'm more comfortable with fiction. Yet the essay form is tempting, given its digressive nature. In recent years, creative or literary nonfiction has drawn me towards the essay, to play with 'mindscapes' (mental landscapes that are both escapist and factual): to examine my writer's life in all its impossible mystery. 'BG: The Significant Years' began from my twin obsessions with the stock market and time. Trading stocks and futures filled my daily rice bowl after I left corporate life in 1998 to live the writer's life. Obsession with time was, however, a longer-standing one, perhaps best expressed in T.S. Eliot's *Four Quartets*, particularly 'Burnt Norton'; I am haunted by Eliot's rose garden, behind 'the door we never opened', and continue an erratic search for it. These two obsessions, coupled with the insoluble mystery for any artist of why and how a work emerges, gave birth to my before-and-post-Google 'calendar'. The concept of the calendar is slippery, and research around the history of calendars simply provided further evidence of the absurdity of measuring time. It is this knowing and not knowing that is the heart of the creative process, and was very WrICE. Abandoning what we think we know is the path into not-knowing, and startling discoveries can emerge for our work. At WrICE Vietnam, I had a breakthrough on my stalled novel, 'The Milton Man'. Everything I'd imagined about my protagonist proved wrong, and by tapping into my unconscious I was able to unearth my *real* Milton man. To echo the painter Francis Bacon — *well, there it is.*

TREATISE ON POETRY

Nyein Way

(I) An Introduction

A: The whole series of life is a train of
executive history in the flash moments of a diving
into the most flooded area in a greasy
mind. What do you think?

B: The death of the intellectual jealousy starts
at the birth of simplicity in relation with the
thought, afterthought and immediate acts
upon the declaration of the self-imposed
arena of the nonfictional translation in a
more — than — one — life — of — laughters —
of — poetics — of — laughing in a distilled
reality of the — truths — now.

C: I can't encounter with the — truths — now
— symptoms on my skin as there is no
gender in lines of poetry.

Nyein Way, the poet, writes: the most shadowy
sorrow in the
world is that of knowing the happiest moments
in the saddest waves in life. Language is
never born with the wind. The most pretentious
music in the world is the twisted lanes in
the most housed wander in pains.

Why are you writing the lines, the words,
the poetry, the text? Is someone
speaking poetry or is he or she writing
texts? Life is so simple that we are
breathing and we are living well. The
cultural and alchemical ends of the cyber physique ideas
are all the beginnings.

Breathe the simplicity of foods in the
rainforest. Create a zone of poetic involvement,
which cannot be signified enough to voyage
the social criticality of the sub-consumed
picture of the writing boat in the air.
Navigate the surrealism of the realist's
inner outfit of the well-designed life pounded
out of the unexpected illusion of freedom.

Fig in the snowy mornings of the gloomy.
Sundays on edge. The cutting-edge idea alumni
has been hiding in the dust in the wind
for a poem of the post-liberated arena
of the circles on the wallpaper.

Mist-Mist. Mist. Rain. Rain. Rain.

The ring has come out of a reading panel
marching towards the vanity fair of the ordinary
colours. Inside out. Outside In. Mix. Mix. Mix.
I love the purest form of the culture and the arts.
A dynamic left over.

(II) The Body

Mornings after the flat sleeping upon the
wild call of the tamest zone of lights
on the pane of the refined dusts.
There are three lines in life patterns:
(a) the line of the present life
(b) the line of the past life
(c) the line of the future life
and
the body is the conceptual mapping
cuts appeared on the stamped circulatory
circles of the machinery culture.

Next mornings are lulled into the
smiles of the walls. Leaves are thrown
into the boiling wisdom of the violin.

The knight of the skin-choreography is cultivating
the layers of the blindfolded truths in the
Nile river of the driest thought rolling
on the conscious flow of the realists'
markings on the road to liberal dialogues.

interrupted music calls upon the
opening ceremony digested enough to take
over the unveiled fruit.

The lice of the brightest flowers are
burning like a mouse on digital
culture of the literary genius.

The repetition has begun to transform
into the circulation of the beginning
with no ends.

Slippers, umbrellas, and grasslands in the
dreamlands of the long-standing queue on
the wind-blown back of the voyager.

This is a soft life. The subtle understanding
of the event in the suite of the adventurers is
being Lawned. The black is stopped. The white.

Life is actually a machine. Life is actually a
method. Life is actually a poem. Life is
actually an aesthetics of the neuro-aesthetics. Poetics of
  a machine.
Life is a machinery of the world. Life is a
picture of a collaged truth. Believe it or not.

Skins of the pretentious flesh and bone of
the lies. The feast of the stopping poem.
The laws of the Lawns in the beam.

A tarred slip into the grasp of the
strengthening string in a skilful harp of the
flies in vain.

Being overcautious of being a poem kills a
poet as a poem is always free as a bird
with colourful wings and monotoned shapes.

Joycean realities on paper are skinned towards
the realisations of the forwarded para-nothingness
into the abyss of the flesh on the pens.

This is a pen you are holding as a ship
of fools flying into the sowing machines of
the impermanence.

All the wings are mused with the chaotic sounds in the
carpeted illusions spreading over the maintenance of the
treatise on poetics
Difficult to understand it? Difficult to
pronounce it? Sound familiar? Strange? Where is
the ladder of luck?
The lovely tree in the forest dissolving into the
time and space of the open imagination; the
reality in the arrow
of the speedy communication pattern which is
being cultivated in the plantation of the
marginalised freedoms.
The breeze is bouncing out of the star on edge
searching for a place to tell a story of the
decamping silence.
The tide colours the hilly children
where there are so many forested insights touching
upon the sounds of the running steps.
The red light before the zebra crossing Nobody is
shouting. The files of the night are marching
towards the fired sleeps
The serious music of the mightiest screen is the
depth of the recurrent energy
of the circulatory map.

The map of the method of the meaning this
piece of writing is that of
'the dark reading', the brightest darkness in senior moments.

Memories of the running water sloping towards the body
of the physical training can be shown but it cannot be
inscribed. The poetry of life
is something like that of the running man climbing up
the hilly formations of mind.

      No poetry. No happenings. No words.

      No language. No actions. No behaviours.

      No lies — No truths. No nowness.

Sometimes Always Rarely. Usually Adverbs
are adverbs on paper.
No future. No present.
Just writing. Touching sense in body.
Thinking is a riverlet.
The skin is thin enough to swim across the
beams of an enormous pond in
the brightest hours of the darkness in
whiteness or the luckiest
hours of the whiteness in darkness. Twinned
realities are burning desires of the coughing
zone in a
meanest mountain — earth — I am
rolling upon the fish swimming underneath the
colours. The white. The red. The orange The green.
The auburn. The brown.

The pale. The weak. The strong. The
definitive infinity.

(III) A Conclusion to a Beginning

Innovation is the circulation of the
beginning seed to sing
> A moon walking upon the layers of the sky
> A trusteeship committee of the poetic truths
> Touching the heartbeats inside the head

When you are running, you sometimes forget
you are carrying a body with a destination.

NW: 'Treatise on Poetry' is a journey into my memory, imagination, and thoughts on life in a time of struggle — struggle in mind, in society, and in society in mind. All the symbols and signs have appeared in my mind as memories of physical images, without any assigned meanings, though with some meanings made by society. The apparatus of the meaning-making system in the poet has been deconstructed by the biological and natural energy of the mind–body relationship, the culture of moments, and in my decisions for writing on space. The poetic culture has been designating meanings of life in Space Station 54 (my life age), and lives of meanings on time-station, on moment-to-moment thought-afterthought-thought, on the speediest digital poetry of today's world out of interdependence upon the poet's mind-trans-realities-decision-knowledge-of-the-world-and-skills-for-life-in-actualities. The WrICE program was a wonderful and integrative experience. It gave me the chance to meet with very good writers from Vietnam, Singapore, the Philippines, and Australia. We had the opportunity to listen, learn, and have friendly discussions. We had a good atmosphere and time to write, too. It was a precious time in my life.

THE
NEAR
AND
THE
FAR

SOME HINTS ABOUT TRAVELLING TO THE COUNTRY YOUR FAMILY DEPARTED

Laurel Fantauzzo

It's all right if you don't quite know why you're doing this. There are some vague terms at work here: *connection, identity, hunger, longing* — innumerable, ungraspable et ceteras. Feel your anxiety. But defy your hesitance, and obey your need to go.

When you arrive, some ghost feeling will enter your lungs along with the air. Somehow you'll recognise this smell. The olfactory accumulation of tired air-conditioning units, standing water, perpetual sweat. Traces of exhaustion and pulsation. To you, it will not be a bad smell. It will remind you of your family for reasons you will never be able to explain.

The country won't embrace you the way you secretly want it to. Unless you mean the heat, which will grip you intimately, like an unwelcome relative.

You won't feel immediately at home. You'll feel immediately motion sick. The stop-and-go, homicidal-suicidal transport, the street-side folks who never stop staring at you, the streams of sweat you never knew you could sweat, the new acquaintances who laugh at tragedies and make dirty jokes to cope. You'll do a lot of awkward smiling, a lot of wishing you were in bed.

You'll get sick, sicker than you thought possible. You'll sit in the lobby of an emergency room waiting for the results of your blood test. A young woman your age, training to be a nurse, will say she's also having LBM, an acronym you don't yet know stands for *loose bowel movement*. She'll ask what you do, and you'll say, grimacing, 'I'm a writer.'

'Ah! Like Clark Kent,' she'll reply, and then she'll tell you all about having had her LBM for a few days now. She's like a newfound cousin in your shared ailments. You'll leave the hospital with her email address and a handful of antibiotics, forty US dollars total for the visit.

You know the only thing that will make you feel better? McDonald's chicken nuggets. Yes, your body is indeed as weird as you think.

When you're finally healthy, take cabs to the malls for the air conditioning. Walk the glamorous grounds of Greenbelt 5. Gawk at the near-empty stores selling Coach and Lacoste. Meet friends in downtown Makati, the business district kept fanatically clean by hundreds of low-wage workers for white-collar workers and insomniac call-centre agents at multinational companies. Follow the lead of the rich locals and dodge the dirty kids selling white strings of fresh sampaguita flower blossoms.

Then, get out of Makati. Get out of the cabs. Get out of the air conditioning. Go to Quezon City. Get on a jeepney. Get on a bicycle.

You'll learn that the unpredictability of the weather is the Philippines' great equaliser. Rich and poor folks alike are at the weather's mercy: its heat, and especially its storms. Everyone is eventually stranded. Learn to live in the weather, to wait for its departure and arrival. Learn to prefer the manual fan over air conditioning. The cold is so unnatural here.

You'll meet certain non-Filipinos who will look at your dark hair and your relatively pale face and hear your American accent, your *r*s and vowels from California, and they'll decide you're one of them. You'll feel that internal tug, that internal rebellion, that pain that arises whenever one side tries to claim you. Then these people will start to talk a lot.

They'll tell you the customer service here is just terrible. And the transportation is deadly, just deadly. They'll grumble that everyone here in the Philippines is just trying to take advantage. That housing is corrupt, business is corrupt, corruption corruption, god, someone has to come clean this place up. And the swaggering undercurrent is *duh*, the cleanup won't come from the messed-up, childish, half-formed locals. It'll come from the capable outsiders, like them. Like you.

Never mind that they share the history of the outsiders who proudly looted and commanded and plundered the islands, calling their own crimes 'progress'.

You'll be uneasy. You'll feel some free-floating guilt. You'll think of your own white dad, how he'd nod and nod in agreement if he were here. You'll want to yell, 'Coloniser redux!'

You'll learn that these non-Filipinos will not hear your hostility, because they can only hear their own certainty.

But sometimes you'll feel your non-Filipino-ness keenly. You'll ask, *Which self am I?* You'll feel too *other*, too intrusive. In your despair, you'll feel like a coloniser yourself. *Am I one?* you will ask. *Am I?*

Well. It depends. When you speak too quickly and too demandingly, or when you lose your temper at a cab driver or a shopkeeper or a new acquaintance or a new teacher or an administrator or a security guard going too slowly or indirectly or complicatedly for you, maybe you are.

When you notice your gracelessness during those moments, close your mouth and listen.

Listen to the director of Filipino indie films who misses his young, murdered friends.

Listen to the wealthy heir to a corporate fortune, beholden to her parents' expectations forever.

The cab driver who hasn't been able to eat for twenty-six hours. And yes, dammit, give him your leftover chicken nuggets.

Listen to the environmental activist, tired from the death threats from mining corporations, who nods off over her newspapers at four in the morning after making resigned jokes about said death threats.

The cheerful survivors of Martial Law, whose torturers are politicians and businessmen now. Listen to them laughing about running into their torturers on the train, seeing them making speeches on television.

Read as much as you can about Martial Law. Your mother refused to tell you about it, yelled at you whenever you asked, since her friends died and police were looking for her and her father burned her protest pamphlets and you seemed always so ready to tap some pain she didn't want tapped. So leave your mother alone and read instead.

When you meet your cousins for the first time, a quintet of men in their mid-thirties, you won't see or feel any resemblance at all. You're of a paler hue, as always, and you can't keep up with their Tagalog jokes. Then these unfamiliar men will hold out their limbs. You'll see that you share the same skinny ankles, the same skinny wrists.

Always carry tissue paper, an umbrella, hand sanitiser, and a handkerchief.

The Filipino style of the indirect answer — the 'no' without saying 'no' — will never cease to make you feel nervous. Pause. Breathe through these moments. Consider what is said and what is left unsaid. Words and the absence of words both carry volume and weight.

When you feel stressed out — and good Christ, you will feel stressed out — do what Filipinos do. Eat.

Eat taho, the warm, sweet, fifteen-peso morning snack you keep hearing men call out mournfully on your street. *Taho. Tahooooooo.*

Eat mangoes. Ever tasted a part of the sun before? That's what a mango is.

Eat balut. Despite all Western scorn heaped on this fermented duck egg, to you it's purer than the hot dog — a salty, amalgamated mystery meat. At least balut, curled and soft and ready in its shell, is just one recognisable animal.

You won't really like balut, if you're being honest, but that's okay too.

By the way, coconuts are supposed to be green, not the sad, hairy, brown, industrial muck you have always eaten elsewhere. Find the manong pushing his wooden cart full of green globes. Order one. Watch him crack it open.

Linger at the doorways of churches, smelling the incense, watching the people seated in pews and praying. Turn away.

Have two karaoke songs ready. It doesn't matter if you can't sing. Sing. Everyone here sings, no matter the sorrow, no matter the hour.

Never regard another human as someone underfoot. Not the chauffeur, not the maid, not the homeless child, not the bathroom attendant, not the guard. Look into each person's face. Remember: no one is a mere instrument of your own movement.

Know that you're going to fail at this. After those failures you'll shrink with shame. As you should.

This is a battered and traumatised place. This is a place that will often behave accordingly. This place will demand the most creative empathy you can summon, even when you're confused beyond all language. Summon it. You can, even when you're sure you can't.

And you'll learn the language soon enough, anyway. Your favourite Tagalog word will be alitaptap: 'firefly'. Your second-favourite will be malaya: 'freedom'.

Your third-favourite? Malayo. For 'far away'. Yes, the spelling is close, isn't it?

LF: Like many members of the Filipino diaspora, and like many bearers of mixed-race heritage, I occupy an odd perspective and an indeterminate status in whatever society I enter. I challenge the racial imaginations of Australians, Americans, and Filipinos alike. In Eastern Europe, strangers asked if I was from China or Korea; in California, shopkeepers called out to me in Mexican Spanish. 'What are you really?' is the insistent question, when I try to give a full and accurate account of my ethnic and racial heritage. On some days the interrogation of my identity exhausts me. On other days I feel oddly honoured that I so challenge the racial imaginations of most countries' citizens. Every day I find my own liminality a rich location to write from. Easy resolutions aren't healthy for nonfiction writers, after all; the nature of the essayist is to feel a restless grappling with impossible questions. At WrICE, gathering with black, Indigenous, and white Australians alongside Singaporean, Malaysian, and American writers, I felt I could inhabit my own complex self in a complete and comfortable way. Each member and leader of WrICE accepted me as a fellow hyphenated traveller in a world too often riven with binaries. In between drafts of an essay about my mother's homeland, I scribbled bits of this piece by hand: things I would have wanted my anxious past self to know about forming a relationship to the Philippines. It encompasses many of the fears and challenges mixed-race and third-culture children might feel at encountering the homeland their parents left behind.

THREE POEMS

Nguyen Bao Chan

The Train of Time

The sunlight hurries
the rain rattles
they are together
on the obsessed train of time
I am in the middle of the year
the month
my life
I am among the trees
the dust
and human beings
I don't know when I boarded this train
here is my thirteen-year-old face
it looks as pure as the early morning dew
here is my twenty-year-old face

it looks as radiant as the sunlight
and here, a still face of the forties
my present is this
the greatest storms may have abated
some afternoon's quietness resting
in an empty garden
from which the leaves have been swept away
I see my dear friends' faces
filled with joys, pains, happiness, sorrow
their children born, growing up,
as dense as the young forests
there have been little seeds
that have never sprouted
the green sleeps forever
in hidden dreams
I see the face of my man
his brilliant forehead
drawn with the trails of thought
I have survived one
and been lost in another
our burning kisses have cooled
our overflowing tears have dried
I don't know why
when someone has left the train
the next seat still remains warm
one's word has been given
but the old station has stepped away
I see my father

precariously moving towards peace

I see my mother

alone, going upwind

her blouse tails are like fragile sails

filled with sadness

I see my grandmother's shadow

the shape of a coloured cloud

beyond the rainbow

vanish into nothingness

Time passes

will there be anyone left

on this obsessed train?

21 June 2011

Missing

Leaves are absent from the trees

Clouds are missing in the sky

The sun longs for the figure of Spring

coming with green buds

Someone has left

The season has gone

carrying traces of the birds

those left on grey-tiled roofs,

pass by the corner of my eye

A hasty flapping sounds in my chest

My heart wants to escape,

fly away with the birds
to a green place of young leaves
where a home opens to welcome us
with hot tea
Steam covers the lip marks in our cups
The furniture is filled with the smell of the past
When the hands of the clock intimately
hold each other
at midnight
time can hardly breathe

Have you heard the wings in my heart?
When you come back
I might have gone
the trees have no more leaves
the sky no more clouds
the chest empty
Only the traces of birds
forgotten on grey-tiled roofs
and in tearful eyes as well

Please make the old clock run again, Darling!
And light your cigarette
with the burning marks of my lips ...

11 April 2014

Forest

For my literary companions at the Writers Retreat in Strathvea

We sat quietly
round the fireplace
in the sitting room
with our own jumbled thoughts
The flames were sighing in the chimney
The parrots were arguing outside
on the trees
The melancholy leaves of Winter
tried to be as green as they could be
as if they were saying something …

We sat quietly
in the sitting room
among the old pieces of furniture
made in 1915
or even older
From which forest did this ashwood table come?
Who knows
But the wooden veins told us in whispers
about the lives of trees
The forests were alive hundreds of years ago …

We sat quietly
in the sitting room
our thoughts fidgeted
kept constantly moving
They seemed to be lonely planets
turning round and round themselves
Sometimes they met each other
Smiled and said hello
They argued sometimes
And sometimes they indifferently passed each other by ...

We sat quietly
in the sitting room
Thoughts silently sprouted
growing from our lives
And then,
at every single minute
young forests were born
again and again

18 August 2015

NBC: A new spring is coming to Hanoi, knocking on my door with whispers of sunshine, winds, leaves, and flowers ... Time flies. Many seasons have carved their marks in my life with sadness and joy, disappointments and hopes ... my poetry comes from those traces that remind me so much of every single moment of life that I have experienced. And I am happy to share my life with whoever allows me to enter their souls with love and understanding. It was my great honour to be part of WrICE in 2015. This opportunity gave me many chances to share my experiences of writing with others during our times together in Hoi An, Hanoi, and Melbourne. It enriched me with deep emotion and good memories that might have already been poetry themselves. Actually, these three poems were accidentally chosen as a way of contributing some of my works to the WrICE anthology. As I re-read them, I found that they seemed to link well even though they were written across a span of five years. So, they are fated to appear together in this book. The final poem, 'Forests', one of my newest pieces, is dedicated to my dear literary friends whose works have inspired me so much. I have entered into their 'forests' to find my own, which has endlessly been growing, greening. Please follow me on the train of time, passing through some old paths, from past to future. May you find some traces of yours there, too.

UNMADE IN BANGKOK

David Carlin

1

She puts her face towards the mirror, offering it up to its reflection. If she gets too close, it all becomes blurry. She has a stick (she realises too late that she doesn't even know what this stick is called), an unmarked cylinder that has seen better days. Everything about the thing is beige and this is perfect because its purpose is to conceal. Her skin is bad. This writing of herself in the third-person feminine is surprisingly hard, as if she were walking into a strong headwind. The urge to turn around/turn over/go back across is almost unbearable to resist. It makes her dizzy. It stops each and every word in its tracks. Each sentence emerges thick and viscous —

Focus on the mirror. She has shaven earlier with a broken razor. In this October Bangkok hotel room the shower is also broken. She wants to recount these details, even if she's not sure of their significance. On the edge of the shadow of her moustache, at ten o'clock to her kisser (as if this topographic accuracy could possibly matter), the first red spot appears. Above, across her cheeks and nose, red swatches are embroidered with pimples large and small. Her skin betrays her. She pops the top off the stick and dabs.

If she writes thus, with the feminine shooshing of the she-voice, is she already made-up, even before the application of the beige wand in her hand?

2

Coming to Bangkok for the first time, a naïve Westerner notices *ladyboys* everywhere. The ladyboy, or *kathoey*, culture in Thailand runs long and deep: there aren't exactly tourist posters at the airport (not yet), but it's certainly not hidden. Ladyboys, thinks the naïve Westerner — who in this case, as fate would have it, is straight and, furthermore, *cisgendered* (as against *trans-*, you see) — look as if they were trying to pass as females going about their daily business. Born into what appears to be a male body and still carrying signs of that chromosomal marker about with them, more or less (with or without the benefit of chemical or surgical intervention), they adopt some selection of the contemporary surface signs of femaleness: clothes, make-up, jewellery, accessories. Here, to say the least, there is a lot of choice.

After a while one begins to notice the counterparts of the *kathoey* in gender crossing: those who would have been announced at birth as girls and packed off (figuratively or literally) to the pink room (if pink means pink in Thailand?). How different is this trajectory, looking only at its visible effects. Where *kathoey* must dress *up* to pass as women — or as *sao praphet song* ('a second kind of girl'), or even as *phet tee sam* (third sex/gender) — Toms dress *down*. Typically one might see them working in service jobs, say behind the counter at a café, or as an usher at a cabaret venue downstairs at one's slightly-faded-but-still-making-an-effort hotel. They wear plain black or grey T-shirts and trousers, like all the other men. Their hair is trimmed short and plain, like all the other men. Their breasts are, if necessary, strapped down, squeezed into the background, nondescript. This attention to detail mirrors the disappearing act of the bikini-clad ladyboy, taping her penis back between her legs.

To become a woman even today, it would appear, is a pantomime of sorts, or at least an intricate performance with, at the centre of its artificial logic, the baroque. To become a man, by contrast, is to tone down, deflect the gaze. None of this is news, but seeing it played out so commonly and openly in Bangkok has the benefit of returning the performance of gender to its rightful queerness.

In any street, out any window, one can't help but scan the world for fellow humans. Stickybeaking, perving, checking out. Appraising, judging, organising into categories. In Bangkok anybody appearing at first glance — first *heteronormative* glance — to be a woman might be revealed, upon closer examination, to have been born with and possibly still be sporting various bodily legacies of the Y chromosome. And vice versa for the men. Look more closely and the straightforward lines of gender start to melt and sway. Even, if you're lucky, sashay.

3

Meanwhile, something else has happened: Virginia Woolf is loose in the hotel. Although way past old by now, she has evidently acquired the capacity to live outside normal bounds. Like her character Orlando, who turned one day from man into woman but was still very much Orlando. Orlando lived for centuries. Writing *Orlando* gave Virginia the license to walk between genders and across time, and clearly she intends to use it:

'He beheld,' Virginia declaims, 'coming from the pavilion of the Muscovite Embassy, a figure, which, whether boy's or woman's, for the loose tunic and trousers of the Russian fashion served to disguise the sex, filled him with the highest curiosity.'

Virginia has improvised a kind of Speaker's Corner near the lifts on the eleventh floor. A small crowd has gathered: those who, after breakfast, have time to kill; cleaning staff finding things to fuss with on their trolleys in the corridor. Directly after publishing *Orlando*, Virginia delivered a series of lectures that later became *A Room of One's Own*. On the eleventh floor she is now reprising highlights.

'It is fatal to be a man or woman pure and simple; one must be woman-manly or man-womanly ... What is meant by "reality"? It would seem to be something very erratic, very undependable — now to be found in a dusty road, now in a scrap of newspaper in the street, now a daffodil in the sun ... But whatever it touches, it fixes and makes permanent.'

Asked to compose these lectures on the question of women and fiction-writing, as she had been one October some eighty-five years prior, Virginia invoked fiction's license. Her argument was that financial independence, time, and space were the fundamental requirements for a future 'Shakespeare's sister' to emerge. But this treatise was couched within a fictional conceit. It was an avowedly fictional Virginia, a surrogate named Mary (with a variety of surnames), who had spent a couple of days reading, observing, and generally contemplating the topic at hand. This make-up allowed Virginia the greatest possible range of play and artfulness within the confines of the essay form.

Making up an 'I' freed Virginia from the weight of drab 'nonfictional' plausibility, as she skipped through the thought processes of her deliberately sketchy alter ego. What did it matter whether the protagonist's encounters with the various men who refused her entry to 'their' august institutions actually occurred to Virginia herself on a single walk? What did it matter whether these events actually occurred to the author-narrator herself at all, as against being events that could and would certainly occur to any woman at those times and places? Why not don the garb of fiction when it suited?

However, Virginia cautions, from the unstable heights of the eleventh floor, as the Skytrain rumbles by: fiction imposes its own conventions of plausibility. 'As I have said already that it was an October day, I dare not forfeit your respect and imperil the fair name of fiction by changing the season and describing lilacs hanging over garden walls, crocuses, tulips, and other flowers of spring. Fiction must stick to facts, and the truer the facts the better the fiction — so we are told.'

4

She turns back to the mirror and goes about the task of partially obscuring herself with the facial ointment. She wonders: is this what is called foundation? If she were playing her role with more diligence, if she were well-researched rather than relying on improvisation, she would know these things.

Even her pronoun — that which seems in some ways most intimate to her — is a cover-up, an artifice. Is she even now a fictional creation, merely by virtue of this make-up? But making up is not so easily resolved.

We would like to think the world could be divided so: between granite and powder puffs, hard realities, soft fantasies. Dicks and cunts. Everything and everyone in its place, with God the referee and linesman. That's in! That's out! You're out of your mind. What would you know? Get back into your own skin and zip it!

The pronouns are jostling. Some languages don't have this problem. In some languages he and she are all mixed up together, like *they* in English, they who indiscriminately cross genders.

The make-up is in the interest of looking better. Nevertheless she feels the need to hide — not only her unsightly blemishes, but the fact of making up itself. She wants to pass as unmade-up, because this is after all what — men — are. Women make themselves up, men do not. This is curious, when she thinks about it. To be a woman, in this culture, is to be a creature dipped in fiction, whereas to be a man is to be altogether real or at least natural, unconstructed. A woman is assembled, touched up (observe the threat of sexual violence). A man is assembled just as surely, his beard trimmed, his hair combed or ragged. But it isn't manly to be made-up.

5

He steps out into the hotel corridor and nobody takes a second glance.

He passes.

He tries to avoid eye contact in the lift. If there is a woman in there he will check her out, but subtly, within the bounds of polite deniability. He has learnt the art of looking, the invisible powers that attend his pronoun.

He, just as much as she at the mirror, is being made up, making himself up. But he can deny almost anything. What mirror? What preening? What touching up? In order to pass, this is his homework. This is something he was learning even as he learnt to speak.

He is proving, if anything, even more difficult than she was. She came with a staging, a purpose, an activity: overtones of theatricality (the theatre, that liminal zone where it is accepted, almost mandatory, that everything and everyone is made-up). He is stuck, perhaps surprisingly, within a mirrored hotel lift. If alone, he checks himself out. Will he pass? If so, as what? A wanted man, desirable? He retreats into himself. The mask he and she have both learnt to apply is insouciance. Uncaring. A shield from the ceaseless bombard of particles coming at them — pheromones, hormones, endorphins, bad breath, God knows what. He takes advantage of his pronoun, maintains his distance, refuses to be drawn. Only if he has to describe anything that is happening inside him might he come up blank.

At the appropriate time he will step out of the lift affecting confidence, as if none of this has happened. The hotel foyer will be crowded like a Brueghel picture and he will walk straight through the middle, seemingly transparent.

6

Let him go, she thinks. He was becoming a trifle boring anyway. So terribly straight-backed, backed by straightness. She, on the other hand, is settling in. She is only now realising how appropriate it is to be lingering in a hotel, of all places. Here, she is anything but alone. In fact, Virginia is at the foyer bar drinking Scotch and discussing Heidegger with an essayist called Wayne Koestenbaum, who fancies hotels. 'Not-being-at-home', she overhears Wayne saying, is, according to Heidegger, a more 'primordial phenomenon' than being-at-home. Adrift here, she considers this. The hotel, Wayne is saying, is the epitome of *not-at-homeness*, a place for checking in and checking out, a transitory place for the *shiftless*. He confides to Virginia, sotto voce: 'I'm impersonating Heidegger to create a language that will serve as my hotel room. One way to be an "I" is to lose the "I". I lose my "I" in the hotel.'

Too right, she thinks, she too has lost her 'I', here in

the hotel. She has put down her 'I'; it's almost as if she has mislaid it somewhere, hoping to discover something else, she knows not quite what, and despite being completely done up as a man.

'Pretend that "hotel" is a verb,' Wayne continues, on a heady roll. 'To hotel is to engage in practices of incremental self-repair'— he picks out each word like a shiny M&M — 'to improvise such practices; to forget and reinvent them.' What is he saying? Hotel mending, respite care for the soul? Virginia politely takes her leave.

This all needs digesting, as anything remotely connected to Heidegger most probably would. She wonders idly what would happen to Wayne's sentence if the verb 'to hotel' were replaced by the verb 'to essay'. Like Wayne himself, she wants to clash together this marginal pair of verbs, this hotelling and this essaying. But while Wayne is after self-repair, she is interested in self-dismantling. Can the essay help us think by building systematic practices of both self-repair *and* -dismantling — improvising, forgetting, re-inventing? Is this what she is trying to do? She feels immensely clever for a moment.

The hallucinations, if that's what they are, proceed. Michel de Montaigne, who inevitably turns up for a free drink whenever the word 'essay' starts to be thrown around, is now propped up at the bar beside Wayne. As befits his generation, Michel is wearing sixteenth-century garb. Even though his mother tongue is Latin, he speaks now in a strangely French-accented English, as if overdubbed: 'There is no desire more natural than the desire for knowledge. We try all the ways that can lead us to it. When reason fails us, we use experience.'

Experience. This is exactly how she began, in front of the mirror that afternoon in the hotel bathroom with the beige concealer and the sudden appearance of the two words 'making up', as if written on the glass with lipstick. This is the personal experience she now spirals out from, eddying towards a kind of knowledge. As Adorno once said, to essay is to be methodically unmethodical. Like the motion of a swizzle stick in a cocktail at happy hour.

She finds herself sitting in a large lounge chair in the foyer, crossing her trousered legs. What is she becoming? Ever more fictional? A character in drag? As if conjured by the word *drag*, another sage appears, the philosopher Judith Butler (perhaps they are all on a post-postmodern package tour somewhere?). 'In imitating gender,' Judith murmurs, 'drag implicitly reveals the imitative structure of gender itself.' Her listener leans in. 'Drag,' says Judith drily, 'brings to the surface and makes legible there the distinctness of those aspects of gendered experience which are falsely naturalised as a unity through the regulatory fiction of heterosexual coherence.' Drag! It is as if a hundred doors are opening somewhere in the hotel, a hundred parties starting. She wants to italicise and em dash Judith's every word! What an apt and ominous phrase: *the regulatory fiction of heterosexual coherence.* Against her will, she sees an image of a bare-chested Vladimir Putin, a gun across his lap. But of course, the whole thing's much more subtle. In the *actual* world we live in, our lives are regulated by the *fictions* of coherence and normality, which we perform or resist, or both.

But who are 'we', all of a sudden, she wonders in the foyer?

7

My body, pale and flat, is only revealed in public on the edge of the rooftop hotel pool. A couple of young tourists attempting to sunbathe in the afternoon haze show no interest. Neither does the woman tasked with dispensing towels, bored in her booth with a magazine. I might as well be invisible.

8

Later that evening he accompanies a friend to the cabaret show in the basement theatre of the hotel. As they walk across the foyer, a Thai man made up as Elvis is singing *I did it my way* in the breakfast bar, accompanied by a CD and an amplifier. A sign says that the Thai Elvis also does Tom Jones and Engelbert Humperdrinck (sic), always between 7.30 and 9 p.m., except on Sundays. This hotel, in fact, has almost everything, even if it seems quite possible that none of it is real.

He and his friend are the only people descending to the theatre. The staircase is lined with large-scale photographs promising onstage spectacle and colour. Two black-T-shirted ushers meet them at the bottom of the stairs. *Toms*, his friend points out, knowing that he is interested. He blinks and notices.

It is a sad night for the theatre. There are no more than ten people in the audience, scattered among the empty seats, but on stage there are twice as many, once the curtain draws back to reveal the opening number. The show is all singing and all dancing, if singing can be understood as miming, that gloriously full-throated form of counterfeit.

One of the Tom-ushers brings the vodka and tonic included in the ticket price. On stage a girl belts out 'River Deep — Mountain High', but silently. A boy mimes 'Mr Bojangles'. Dressed like a minstrel, he also mime-strums the guitar while another boy camply improvises arabesques and pliés. The ladyboys in the ensemble play it straight like all the other girls, or so he thinks, before he discovers he has made up this distinction and all the other girls are ladyboys as well.

So as to remember things, he takes videos with his smart phone.

At the end of the show, the performers line up hastily on either side of a mirrored corridor in their sequins, feathers, and chiffon. Come! They reach out. Come and stand with us for photographs! Their skin is glistening with the sweat of dancing. He is tempted. He stands between two girls with dancers' legs. In the photograph, he looks starkly middle-aged, and his skin is bad again. The make-up isn't working.

He steps out of the picture. You give me money, the girls say, suddenly urgent. You got your picture. You give me money! They've done two shows tonight; they need to pay the rent. He fumbles for his wallet.

9

Have you noticed: all the hotel guests are white? All the philosophers, the writers. The Asians are the anonymous workers in this story, serving vodka, folding towels, performing gender, providing metaphors, being Elvis. For a long time, all afternoon and evening, this has just seemed normal here at the hotel. The regulatory fiction of *monocultural* coherence, pale-faced half-truths and all that.

But actually, Elvis is a man named Jaruek Viriyakit.

Jaruek is his own man. He only comes in between 7.30 p.m. and 9, and is unavailable for literary use outside those hours.

10

She closes the door of the hotel room. Washes her face in the bathroom sink. Make-up smudges beige across the white towel.

What has she discovered? Where would such a discovery be located? In the gap between her and him? In the smudge of colour on the towel?

Now, in front of the mirror, not for the first time, s—h—e disintegrates.

All is darkness.

But after a moment, there is a knock on the door. Someone has come to fix the shower. Even more surprisingly, it is Hélène Cixous, the French writer. 'Virginia sent me,' she says, and closes the door. Getting out her tools, she remarks, 'When we say to a woman that she is a man or to a man that he is a woman, it is a terrible insult.' She shrugs, waving a heavy wrench suggestively. 'This is why we cut one another's throats.'

S—h—e doesn't know what to make of this.

So Hélène continues, philosopher as plumber: 'We have extremely strong identifications, which found our house.'

S—h—e, thinking immediately of Wayne, is moved to interject: 'But this is not a house, it's a hotel. Anything can happen here.'

Hélène continues on, regardless: 'An *identity* card,' she says, 'doesn't allow for confusion, torment, or bewilderment. If the truth about loving or hateful choices were revealed it would break open the earth's crust. Which is why we live in legalised and general delusion.'

She pauses and does something marvellous with the wrench.

'Fiction,' she concludes, 'takes the place of reality.'

Some fictions trap us. Comfort us, yes, delude us. Bully us, or others, into shapes and voices.

But other fictions free us. A hundred doors are opening somewhere in the hotel, a hundred parties starting. Outside there are firecrackers. Really.

Away from the mirror, s—h—e can't tell what their skin looks like.

Hélène gazes up at the shower rose. Bangkok water falls on them both, and they are unmade.

—————————————

DC: The personal essay is usually the province of the 'I' — it is the 'I' that puts the person into the personal and shows us a vision of the world as filtered through the essayist's unique net of experiences, thoughts, emotions, and inheritances. This essay came about from wondering what would happen if the 'I' of the essay became a 'he' — easy enough, it turns out, for a cis-gendered male essayist — but then, too, to go a step further away, a 'she'? At this point, everything started to bend in much more interesting ways. I wanted to explore the cracks in what seems normal about how we compose ourselves as boys or girls, males or females. It is no coincidence that these thoughts surfaced somewhere a long way from home: Bangkok, where cultural traditions, committed activism, and exploitative sex tourism combine to make transgender identity more visible than in many other places. Transgender people are at the forefront of thinking about how gender identities and bodies are made and remade, but these are questions that shape and define us all, it seems to me, whoever we may be.

COMADRONA

Jhoanna Lynn B. Cruz

I had come to Ilocos Sur looking for my father. No, not him but his family, for I had only his mother's name, Sibayan. My mother had forgotten which town. She said it had been too long ago, and she too old to remember such trivial details. I had one week off from work to scour the municipal files of each town, from Tagudin to Vigan. The journey led me only to Lumen. Which was just as well. Perhaps.

I had heard of the Vigan clay jars called *burnay* and wanted to buy one for my mother, knowing how sore she would be if I didn't bring her any pasalubong. It was Good Friday. I had a feeling the factory would be closed, but I drove by anyway, just in case.

I saw her sweeping the yard, with the yellow leaves of the sampaloc trees falling like soft rain. Some leaves caught in her curly hair, carelessly tied in a bun. The sight reminded me of weddings: the way the couple is showered with petals and rice grains as they leave the church. Charming. She had already started a fire with coconut fronds. The aromatic smoke made a screen for the sunlight filtering through the trees. Most noticeable were the coffee-coloured jars of different shapes and sizes scattered around the yard. The gate was closed, but I called her attention anyway. 'Manang, naimbag nga aldaw!'

She looked up and said, 'Sorry, we're closed.'

I was sure my Ray-Bans gave me away. She seemed irritated to see another tourist.

I persisted and tried to convince her to let me in, which was difficult because I didn't know much Ilocano. Actually, I thought she might be disarmed by my silly effort to speak the language. I hoped that her business sense would overcome her religiosity, but I didn't want her to think that I had no respect for the day of Christ's crucifixion.

She was a stubborn woman, so I climbed the low gate, sat on top of it, and lit a cigarette. I was glad I was not wearing my usual stockings and heels.

Halfway through the cigarette, she finally motioned for me to come down. I knew I had only to match her stubbornness and she would relent. My years as an advertising executive had taught me that.

Up close, I saw that, though she was not very pretty, she had lovely eyes, black as wet coal. On an impulse, I reached out to flick some leaves off her hair. She jerked away like a frightened cat and my fingers touched only the curls that fell on the right side of her face. Gaining control immediately, she held me in her steady gaze and said, 'Please be quick.'

It was difficult to make a choice. There were hundreds of jars. This must be how God feels when He looks upon His creatures and wonders how each one can be so different and yet so alike because we are fashioned from the same clay.

I went around the display area twice. Seeing that she was watching me, I finally chose a tall one with rings around it. I loved it even when I discovered a crack on its body that could not be repaired.

I showed it to her and haggled for the sake of haggling. 'Fifty pesos, manang. Look! It has a crack.'

'I'll give it to you for eighty pesos. If you don't like the price, leave.'

I wondered why she was so impertinent but remembered she was an Ilocana, after all. I almost left just to spite her, but I wanted that jar so I handed her one hundred pesos. As she wrapped the jar in old newspapers, she muttered to herself, 'It is the brokenness that makes it beautiful.'

I felt a dreadful desire to know this woman, to probe the brokenness that taught her to value this jar the way I did. In my mind, I heard my friends warning me against my folly: 'No, Eva! Go — take the jar and go!' It had only been three months since that other woman had finally dumped me to go back to her perfect marriage. Since then, my friends had had to endure my drinking, my crying, my endless soliloquies.

It was fair warning. I knew their voices were right. Instead, I removed my shades, sat on a big jar turned upside down, and asked for her name.

'Do you know that these jars will not break under your

weight because they go through the fire twice as long as ordinary terracotta pots?' she asked.

'Really? That's good. I hate those signs that go "lovely to look at, nice to hold, but if you drop it, it's considered sold". I never dare touch things that come with such warnings.'

'But the temptation,' she said, suddenly smiling. She then picked up a rock and used it to tap the jar I was sitting on. It produced the clinking sound of crystal goblets. The back of her hand slid past my calf and I sighed inaudibly, thankful that I had just shaved. I wondered if she had meant to touch me. Without dropping her hold on my eyes, she said, 'That's how to tell if it's real burnay. Next time, you should check first. My name is Lumen.'

The way her mouth rounded on the syllables of her name, I felt the sound swirling and echoing in my head. I gave my name to her then, wanting her to take it in her mouth and love it the way I thought she did hers. She did not say my name until that evening in the birthing room.

I told her why I had come to Ilocos and she offered to help me, explaining that her husband worked in the mayor's office and might be able to expedite my search. The voices again: 'No, Eva! Go — take the jar and go!' Instead, I proposed to drive her home.

'All right, but I have to close shop. Will you wait?'

'Even if it takes forever!'

I laughed at how cheesy that line was, knowing that I had opened myself up again to a hopeless situation.

Lumen smiled. 'Nervous laughter?' She walked towards

the fire, which she doused with rainwater stored in a small jar. I noticed that she did not hold her blouse to her chest when she stooped to pick it up.

On the way to her house, she asked me to drive around the plaza. She pointed at the building right beside the Arzobispado and said, 'St Paul College. That's where I studied.'

'Exclusive girls' school?'

'At that time but not anymore.'

'My mother sent me to co-ed schools. To prepare me for the real world, she claimed. I probably would have had more fun if I had gone to St Scholastica's!'

'Yes,' she replied.

Their house was on Crisologo Street, not far from the factory. It was a postcard-pretty avenue, with its rows of restored Vigan houses — the original red-clay bricks interspersed with new hollow blocks and cement, the wooden doors still big enough for the entry of carriages. I had read that in the past, the ground floor of a Vigan house was used only as garage, granary, and servants' quarters. The 'real' house was upstairs, to highlight the distance between the inhabitants. The old cobblestone roads had been restored with limestone because it was cheaper and easier to source. Still, the hooves of horses and their carretelas produced a plaintive melody broken only by the intrusive whir of tricycles.

I had never been inside one of these old houses and was jolted by how easily her antiques sat beside the amenities of our time. I loved the sheen and warmth of the capiz-shell windows and how the builders had left untouched some broken squares from which one could peer at the treasures inside. Or outside. But the iron grills were anachronistic.

As if hearing what I was thinking, Lumen explained, without looking at me, 'It was my husband's idea. He thought the grills might deter thieves.'

Looking out the window, I noticed that just across their house was a funeral parlour, with its hearse parked right on the street. I shuddered at the thought of waking up to that scene every day.

The family entertainment system was showcased in antique mahogany shelves that might have been once used for books. In her kitchen were a microwave oven, a fridge, and a freezer. The sink was made of porcelain, and her fish bagoong was still made and stored in burnay jars.

'Why don't you stay and have dinner with us?'

I almost jumped at the opportunity but, to be sure, I asked, 'Wouldn't your husband mind having a stranger in his house?'

'No, not at all. Miguel is fond of entertaining guests, but he'll be late tonight. Rotary Club meeting. I'll make you pinakbet. Kayat mo?' she teased.

'Wen, manang!' I exclaimed, grinning.

I watched her prepare the vegetables for the pinakbet: tarong, parya, otong, okra, kamatis, karabasa. She cut the vegetables in even pieces — so even that it seemed she'd measured and counted them beforehand. The glossy purple of the eggplants was a counterpoint to the bitter green of the wrinkled ampalaya. The orange tint of the squash bounced off the string beans.

When she was done, her fingers were moist with the juice of the okra. I blushed at my desire to take her hands in mine. She sautéed some garlic in a pan and fried the bagnet in its own fat. The hot oil sizzled, and a sinful aroma filled the kitchen. I had to close my eyes, imagining the possibilities. She strained the bagoong in a woven sieve that looked like a dipper.

'If you skip this step, the slivers of fish will ruin the texture of the sauce,' she explained. She then placed the vegetables in a palayok, poured the bagoong into it, covered the pot, and waited. 'The secret to pinakbet is not to use any aluminium utensils to mix. You've got to shake the pot vigorously at the proper time, so the vegetable flavours are mixed without being bruised by the siansi.' She held the palayok firmly with both hands, taking care not to burn herself. She added the bagnet and gave the pot one last shake, then lowered the fire to let the dish simmer while she set the table for four.

I did not have time to wonder because a maid came in just then, carrying a child. Lumen took the boy and sat him on her lap. He had the same head of curly hair and his dark eyes welled with questions.

'My son Niño,' she explained.

'Hello, baby! I'm Tita Eva.'

'I'm not a baby anymore. I'm four years old.' Niño got off Lumen's lap.

'Do you like pinakbet, Niño?' I asked, trying to gain his favour.

'I eat only Mommy's pinakbet. It's the best-best-best! If you eat it, you will never want to leave!'

'You mean like in the kingdom of dwarves?' I sought to hide my sudden urge to walk away while I still could, while I had not yet partaken of the enchanted feast.

'No such thing as duendes, Tita Eva.'

Foiled again, I thought. Lumen laid the bowl of pinakbet on the table. 'All right, mangan tayon!'

I was glad the pinakbet really was the best I'd ever had, so I could gush about it between mouthfuls and not have to talk about what I thought really mattered in this scenario. Husbands were one thing, but children? Watching Lumen with Niño reminded me of those Madonna and Child stampitas we were given during First Communion. I was not sure whether it was right to disturb the finality of such a picture.

After dinner, she gave me a grand tour of the house and pointed out her ancestors in the various portraits hanging in the dining room, which had two huge dining tables made of dark narra and embellished with intricate carvings. I cringed at how much history her family must have in this town where everyone knew everyone. I asked Lumen why there were no portraits of her husband's family, and she blushed. 'They're in the town museum.'

Just then, Miguel arrived. He was a good-looking man, a tall Chinese mestizo with a charming smile. Lumen kissed him on the cheek and introduced us to each other.

Learning about my project, he offered to search the municipal files but explained that he knew of no Sibayans in Vigan.

He asked me where I was staying. When I told him,

he exclaimed, 'Ay Apo, kaasi met! Common toilet and bath! Why would you do that to yourself?'

'I'm just staying overnight anyway. I leave for Manila tomorrow.' I was on the defensive.

'Why don't you stay with us instead?' He put an arm around Lumen. 'Right, honey?'

Looking me in the eye, Lumen answered, 'Yes.'

'Suwerte!' I replied. 'Let me get my things and check out.'

'Sige garud,' Miguel agreed. 'I hope you won't mind if I don't wait up for you. I'm beat.'

In the car, I thought about why Lumen had agreed to have me stay. Experience told me that women like her were unhappy in their marriages and use women like me for entertainment. Miguel was so nice; I almost felt guilty for wanting his wife, but I was too far gone to back out now. I wanted to be inside Lumen.

When I returned to her house, she was holding a key. I thought it surprising because none of the rooms had doors with locks that needed them. Instead, there were large wooden bolts that slid into slots on the doorframes.

'I want to show you where I was born.'

She motioned at me to follow her up the wide staircase. The steps creaked ominously and I remembered a bedtime story an ex-girlfriend had once told me about Bluebeard's last wife and the forbidden room that held his bloody secret.

The birthing room was bare save for a retablo of saints on one wall, right beside the birthing bed. At one end of the room was a bay window that Lumen now opened for ventilation.

She struck a match to light the kingke on top of the camphor chest beside the bed. I marvelled at how burnished her skin was, the same dark earth tones of the burnay.

'Inang gave birth to my father and his five siblings on this bed.'

The bed was made of narra, the wood smooth as glass now because of time and use, its wicker seat curved to follow the contours of a woman heavy with child and angled to reveal the artisan's innate knowledge of the principle of gravity. Its armrests were longer, the ends curled up to accommodate the legs spread wide for the passage of new life.

'In the old days, only women were allowed inside the birthing room and only women assisted in the delivery.' She lay on the birthing bed and stared me in the eye. 'I gave birth to Niño here.'

And this was where I loved her. With a torrent of words, I undressed her, kissed the silver marks on her belly, where her skin had once stretched taut, and sucked on the dark nipples that still seemed to harbour the faint flavour of milk.

I named her body, her beauty to herself. I laved her with promises. My two fingers seemed lost inside her, so I put in one more and still another and yet another. I had never done this before and I was drunk with the exploration.

Kneeling on the floor, my mouth on her open sex, I called to her: 'Come, Lumen. Come. Come.' And thus, she was born, weeping from the shock of being wrenched away from the protective sac, her self-contained world.

'Eva. Eva. Eva.' I was the comadrona.

I held her close to me, prepared to be pushed away. I wanted to ask her so many questions but did not dare.

She cried quietly and said, 'Tell me what you want to hear.'

I did not reply, terrified by what I knew to be the inevitable conclusion to nights such as these.

She took a bead necklace from the baul and gave it to me. 'It's at least a hundred years old. I want you to have it. All my life, I had been taught to want only what was given to me, yet I desired more, something that was truly mine — mine because I wanted it.'

'But you have so much to be thankful for.'

'I do now,' she whispered. 'I think.'

I left for Manila in the morning, before her husband woke. She sent me away with a long string of homemade Vigan longganisa, which reminded me of the rosary project I once tried to make in high school, the one that constantly came undone because I could never twist the wire properly between the decades. How clumsy I had always been with small things.

I gave her my phone number and address because I did not have anything else I thought she might need. She took my hand and kissed it gently four, five times. 'Thank you, Eva.' In her eyes, I saw a faint smouldering that I hoped she would feed with the same devotion she gave to her cooking and her jars. I did not find my father, but it didn't seem to matter anymore.

All I have now is the glass-bead necklace from the camphor chest of Lumen's great-grandmother. She told me it was handcrafted by a Tinguian woman from Abra, who had come to their town bartering her family beads for rice.

Inang, who saw the mud crusting the woman's bare feet and the famine in her eyes, stole a ganta of rice from the family granary and refused the beads, knowing how valuable they were. The woman did not want her charity and left the necklace on the ground. She walked away without looking back, the rice wrapped safely in the cloth sling her people use to carry their babies. The necklace is translucent blue with the memory of sea or sky. It has no clasp to hint of where the string begins or ends. I keep it to invoke what is interminable.

JLC: 'Comadrona' is about a journey taken with specific intentions, which brings forth unexpected gifts. In the story, Eva sets out to look for her father and finds herself a willing midwife to an aspect of Lumen that lay dormant in the life she had chosen. When I received the WrICE fellowship, I had been struggling with the title piece of the memoir I was working on about starting over and coming back to life in Davao City after my marriage failed. I hoped that joining WrICE would help birth this difficult essay. And it did. In Hoi An as well as in Australia, my words flowed. But more than the writing, I found fellowship. In the immersive workshop, I saw how authors at different stages of their careers and from different countries come to grips with the writing process. It was moving to listen to Suchen Christine Lim talk about the eight months after an accident during which she could not move or write. Having taught her stories in my undergraduate classes, I considered it a gift to be privy to her pain and anxiety. Or being in the presence of Cate Kennedy, whose work I had not yet encountered, but whose generosity as a woman and as a writer astounded me. Being with the young, emerging writers reminded me of what it was like to struggle with finding one's voice and story amid the cacophony. It made me feel less alone in the terrible moments of facing the blank page. In the shared space of creative vulnerability, I found a kind of family. When we left Hoi An, the hotel gave each of us a parting gift of Vietnamese pop-up cards. Mine was a cardboard sculpture of a gift box saying 'Happy Birthday'. How apt to make the gifts of WrICE somehow tangible. And like Eva in my story, 'I keep it to invoke what is interminable.'

1:25,000

Francesca Rendle-Short

Elevation and depth

You agree it was a pretty stupid thing to do in hindsight, stand there on a narrow platform of something like two feet of concrete with a freight train barrelling towards you at speed. You and your co-conspirator were between the yellow lines as instructed by the ticket sales person, one behind the other — but still. Trainspotting gone mad. The freight train, one of a hundred or so passing this spot each day in Winslow, Arizona, careened towards you both, engine first. The two of you were riveted to the spot (the others had run away), hearts pumping and screaming your heads off. You waved madly to the driver. You can still feel it now through your body, everything so loud and sort of explosive with wind and noise, weight and volume. In that moment the train and how it was moving towards and in and through you was all there was; it was everything, beyond exhilarating.

Is this a way you could die, she wonders?

Did you ever think to move, someone asks?

Later, police and security men with flashing orange lights and yellow vests summoned the two of you off the track, told you to keep clear. It didn't take them long to get there, either; the train driver must have pulled on the alarm as you were waving. Don't ever do that again, they said. That was very dangerous. Anything could have happened you know (in their sing-song Arizonian drawl).

Index

Before the train incident, you are at Flagstaff, Arizona, up the road and seven thousand feet above sea level and 130 kilometres or so from the Grand Canyon, on a mountain surrounded by volcanoes, including the highest mountain range in the state, the San Francisco Peaks. This is where you want to begin, not far from the Sonoran Desert to the south near Phoenix and the Painted Desert to the east near Winslow (along Route 66, where those hundred trains race by). Flagstaff, nearly as high as Mount Kosciuszko (7,310 feet), the highest peak in Australia, which overlooks Lady Northcote Canyon, where you once said you wanted to be buried, your ashes scattered.

When I die, she said, throw me down here.

She told him as much on a number of occasions when they went cross-country skiing together in the mountains with the kids — these were happy days — the little one in a moulded plastic red sled out the back on long white poles with her collection of soft dolls and stuffed, friendly animals tucked in around her to make a warm nest, the big one more grown up alongside in tandem, elegant on skis.

Tracks

This is an essay on saying no.

On not going to the Grand Canyon.

— *Oh you must go, you'd be crazy not to go.*

— *When will you ever be back in these parts?*

— *It's one of the great wonders of the world.*

— *It will change your views on perspective, on space, on everything.*

On not drinking alcohol (having to say no).

— *Oh really, I don't believe it. Oh, you are so virtuous.*

— *When did you stop drinking?*

— *I always thought you did drink. I can see you with a glass in your hand.*

— *I thought everyone drank in Australia.*

On not writing about him but writing about him nonetheless (American nonfiction writer Phillip Lopate argues that if you write about your life you inevitably write about others).

And on regret.

Gridlines

But she doesn't know any of this before she started. She has to use verbs to help her go, make sentences. *I make it real by putting it into words*, Virginia Woolf said. And this is what she is trying to do. *It is only by putting it into words that I make it whole.*

Tunnel

An Australian writing friend at Flagstaff told you not to go to the Grand Canyon: she said, you couldn't possibly do it justice in such a small space of time, a few hours, even at a glance. Then you read her report of walking in the Grand Canyon the next day in *The Age* newspaper on your phone about the experience of planting herself in the midst of one of the most densely touristed places on the planet over four days and giving in to some greater force — she employs the word *numinous* and you sigh — you are overtaken with such envy, also grief and regret. Why didn't you at least give it a go? Why be so certain (was it that)? What were you thinking — saying no?

You want to feel what it's like to be numinous too.

Highpoint

But then the day of decision comes, a day of clear skies, cool breeze, and the sun warm on the skin, enough for UV protection. A party of nine in two cars sets off to La Posada in Winslow, to the hotel beside that cross-continental Amtrak line. Five of the group go to the Grand Canyon on the way and four don't; they go direct via the Walnut Canyon, as it happens, and the 'largest meteor crater in the world' (which they decide not to visit in the end because of the expense).

You are in that car, the one that doesn't go. All the other three in your car have already seen the Grand Canyon and don't feel the need to see it again, at least not quickly like this, en route.

In the car you are arguing with yourself that your reason for not going was that you wouldn't be able to do it justice. But when the time comes, when it is just about impossible to change your mind, that queasy feeling of regret and sadness sweeps over you. Heart over mind. There's something about that state of desire and longing coupled with determination not to give in that is sort of cool and seductive. It takes you into another zone where you begin to examine everything, where things unravel — what kind of person are you, why can't you just decide and be done with it, would it matter, really, if you changed your mind, why are you testing yourself like this anyway, why can't you have what you want, why not take your cake and eat it, why be so hard? Also: why can't you forget it and just move on?

Covered reservoir

Your girlfriend-partner and one-and-only emails you from Australia about the Grand Canyon (she's a bit glad you're not going there without her; she would have been so jealous). She sends you a quote to appease you and because it's funny, from Irish comedian Ed Bryne — remember him, he did a fabulous sketch on Alanis Morissette, irony, and teaspoons, that had you both in stitches? — Ed Byrne who wears velvet suits and 'clever trousers': 'My problem with the Grand Canyon is Americans are too proud of it for my liking. The Grand Canyon was like that when they found it! And it's not like it was hard to find.'

Ferry route

Needless to say it doesn't help when one of the party in the other car posts a photograph of going 'to the edge of another world', a picture of the poetry of the spatial expressed in a narrow horizontal view of stratified lines in greens and browns and fawns and pinks with the bluest of Arizonian skies above. Even in this limited portrait as expressed on Facebook, you can taste the scale of it, and wonder: its vastness. And the magnificence of the drop — making you keen to fall and soar into the abyss too. Wanting. Missing. Yearning. Longing. Crying out for. Craving. That's mine. I want that too. Another world.

Gauging station

The thing is, when speaking of regret — what with a bearded sage from long ago turning up and asking questions and the scientific oracle talking about falsehoods and poetry — it all comes back to that time, to being planted, as it were, in the garden. Her story of real regret.

She remembers being a younger woman, a married woman in love with a geologist of sorts, a soil scientist — that one whom she's thinking of here in the desert: you'd like this, she wants to tell him. She remembers him taking the call. He was out in the garden in the middle of the day in the shine of the brilliant blue of an Adelaide sky among the pumpkin patch and the tomatoes and beans, that garden he'd built with his own hands from scratch to feed the small family, and she was at the back door, one child on a hip and another at her feet. He was talking to his father. He rang him every week; he was a good son. This particular call was after the first heart episode, the precursor, and she knew his father was dying, they must have both known this, that this was what the call was about, saying goodbye — something about his stance, his bowed head, the clench of his back muscles and fix of his legs, the turnaway face and silence — but she didn't know the exact facts of the matter at that point.

Because, all she can remember in detail is the particular clothes she was wearing while leaning against the jamb, the punk boots and pinched-in waist, and how her soaped-up hair was coiled in a '50s scarf with hatpins.

— *No, we can't go and visit him, she said.*

— *No, it's not on the way.*

— *No, he will have to wait.*

Wreckage

She's never wanted to talk about him, not in a direct way, not like this, but here she is at seven thousand feet above sea level thinking about him, or rather thinking of love, this past love, how it manifests itself — had once revealed itself — and how things can change; how you really can fall in *and out* of love.

Because she wants to tell him about this country, Arizona, the volcanoes, the Sonoran Desert with its tree cactuses and the colours of the Painted Desert of the Badlands. Have a conversation. Has he been here? Does his work on food security and the geopolitics of soil bring him to places like this? She wants to say you'd like this; you used to like this sort of thing, being in country, knowing the ground on which we stand, looking at rock, geological formations, the colour and texture of soil, asking questions, posing hypotheses. Being in the field as a scientist. You would reach out for a sample, roll a bolus, take the pH, give it a name and a type: stratified rock layers, easily erodible soils of sandstone and mudstone, finely grained soil full of iron and manganese compounds, aluminium.

But you're not here.

And she's glad.

Spot height

Writing this, she is in a state of *instar*, that stage between moults, about to slough off the old and slip into a new skin to allow the freshly born to come, *to be there*. That's what writing is, isn't it? Instar, that period of dramatic change that Rebecca Solnit calls 'something both celestial and ingrown, something heavenly and disastrous … oscillating between near and far'.

Fence line

You read somewhere on Google (on a site put together by a 'compass dude' who is mad about maps and symbols): 'Since a map is a reduced representation of the real world, map symbols are used to represent real objects. Without symbols, we wouldn't have maps.'

The symbol of the fence line belongs to someone with a beard, a grey beard puffed out on his chest like the tail feathers of a raptor, who was there at Flagstaff too, at seven thousand feet along with everyone else (you were at a nonfiction conference).

Someone asks: who is that man with the beard? Do you know him? He looks like one of those men out of a fairytale, a mythical creature, a wizard, and a kindly enchanter. He has such an Aussie accent when he asks a question, made more Aussie here in this place, here in Arizona.

This bearded enchanter talks to you. (How long is it since you've seen him?)

— *Has your father died?*

— *I'm an orphan.*

— *Me too.*

— *It's all happened since seeing you last.*

— *And how many years is that?*

— *Over twenty-five I think, maybe thirty.*

— *If we're right.*

— *If we can count.*

And we laugh together like old friends.

Someone else asks:

— *Did you go out with him?*

— *Why do you ask?*

— *He's got a lot of hair.*

We laugh (you don't tell her your once-husband did in fact have a beard).

To be fair, this long-ago friend doesn't ask you about your ex-husband, and you're grateful for that. He's here at the conference to learn about writing too.

Land subject to inundation

You hear from another man too, an enchanter of a different kind, a science wizard when it comes to climate change and knowing about deserts around the world and the way geologies work.

'Science is a search for falsehoods,' this icon declares from the front of the room. 'Scientists have to have imaginations that soar like poets'.'

From the talk around the table, everyone believes him. Why not?

And then over drinks and fresh popcorn you find yourself in a conversation about fathers and about being a father for the second and/or third time. How these men are changing; how they want to be better. You make it sound better too; you make it sound right — make it resonate as normal and good, which it is.

But why do you end up talking to men about being men (about being fathers and sons and lovers) and make them feel good about themselves? And why do you put up with misogynist remarks that make men laugh? Why can't you say no, enough? Is it the altitude?

Blood nose, someone says, it's a sign.

Rocky outcrop

They say if 'acute mountain sickness' gets really bad — you read warnings on Google — you get something called *ataxia*. This means that you can't walk straight, you are feeling very faint, and your breath, your breath that you usually don't take any notice of at all, sounds like a paper bag being crumpled in your ears. If it gets like this, it's deadly.

Abandoned

You hold yourself together with safety pins; keep your smelly armpits to yourself — not like others.

You hope like everyone else that this will all end well.

Contour lines

You like the precision of contour lines, how they can never touch one another. They can't and they never will because that's the rule they must obey by definition, unless and only if it's to mark a cliff such as Lady Northcote Canyon (here contours appear to cross over — but they don't). You also like how topographic contours close in on themselves across the map to make irregular circles. How maps are readable. Dependable. Reliable. Using a map you can get to places you've never been to before.

Man-made feature

Hers was a quick marriage, she was very young, a quick knot (although it lasted many years). It was the fastest there is under Australian law, a six-week timespan between deciding to do it, to finding the celebrant, setting the date, and actually marrying. Her story is that she proposed to him on her knee in the soft dirt at the wooden swing in the park, in pink dungarees, with stolen red roses in her hair. There was no time for her soon-to-be father-in-law to make arrangements to be there: but that didn't seem to matter because he would have wanted to drink whiskey and beer (why not) and her parents were teetotallers — everyone was worried how the bridal parties would mix. The first time she met him was much later, at Christmas, when after lunch she bowled a cricket ball clean across the garden and it smashed through the neighbour's kitchen window as they sat down to eat.

— *Oh no*, she said to her new husband, *do something; please do something.*

But everyone laughed.

Racetrack

You've still got that wedding dress, haven't you, wrapped up in blue tissue in the top cupboard — for what? Nothing can persuade you to throw it away or to give it to Vinnies. But — you say too much. Will you be able to find your way out of this Painted Desert? Follow the map? Find your way home?

> — *Keep drinking, girl.*
>
> — *Don't stop.*
>
> — *You are an older body now than when you started.*

Seepage

Emily Dickinson says:

> — *dont*
> *you know that*
> *'No' is the wildest*
> *word we consign*
> *to Language?*

And somebody says Virginia Woolf says, *Everything is a screen to keep us from noticing too much.*

Dry lake

Her father was instrumental in converting the soon-to-be-husband scientist to Christianity (for a time) but not to creationism, that would have been a bridge too far. (Her father would have called the Grand Canyon *God's Canyon* after his catastrophist views and theory of rapid erosion.) She was married in a cathedral in a university town on the tablelands, her father giving her away in his silk bow tie with her in a heavy white lace dress with a black jersey underneath made by her mother from a lace tablecloth. She made it quickly from scratch in those six weeks; her mother was good with her hands. At the reception they drank sparkling water for toasts. They said they didn't want any presents.

Landing strip

The nonfiction writers inhabiting Flagstaff seem to agree that the answers, if there are any answers, lie in the wide white margins where there is space enough to write your own notes, tell it slant (as Emily Dickinson once famously wrote). This desert is full of white margin.

Altitude

Up here in Flagstaff, the air dries out dirty laundry in the hotel bathroom in the dark overnight, and memories, dry as bone — the smalls: knickers, socks, and pantyhose. But still, this is some slow mapping. You have to drag your body around because of the altitude. You sleep fitfully, but when you do it's a heavy sleep, and your eyes are like sandpaper in the morning, blinking as the sun rises.

Shaded relief

She hasn't thought about him in this way before or in so many words and ways for years, or is it decades? How is it possible that memories inhabit our nervous system, our geologies, long after the passing of that love, and it was a good love too? Something did die in the passing, passed and disappeared. But there was love there once, true love, or as true as it could be at the time, as true as any love can be. So what residue remains? Like wind and rain and geology; like soil. Like sedimentary rock. Like this earth she stands on from the Chinle Formation — there never is any real passing, always residue, always dust.

A still life of a life.

Was it Maggie Nelson who said in one of the nonfiction keynotes: 'We are always experiencing the world experiencing the passage of time.'

Covered reservoir

Her once-father-in-law died not long after that conversation in the garden, may he rest in peace. He had a second heart attack but this time it was fatal. His shop assistant found him alone in his house when he was late coming back to his toyshop after lunch. That garden phone call her husband made was the last conversation he ever had with his father — you need to spell it out to lift it out of the dust. She had said no, let's not go there. Let's wait; think of the kids. She put her foot down but she didn't think he would die. She had never met death before, not like this, not face to face. She didn't know about signs, about that sixth sense people say they get, a sense of foreboding, premonition, and prescience.

She's learnt this the hard way.

Now, if someone feels the need to do something she tells them to follow that instinct and go. Go. She tells herself this also. Don't hold back. Don't say no. Say yes.

Scale

This is an explorer-style map, where every dingle and knoll in the landscape, as they say, is marked in line and dot and colour. Where every measurement is twenty-five thousand times bigger in the real world. This is a slow-going dance of the body, a magnification. The body of thin air and slow breath. A loitering of sorts. *Don't forget to drink plenty of water.*

And when the sun comes up, you open your eyes. Tongue twitching like a frilled lizard, tongue pink, or is it yellow? Some mornings in this place you wake up in a prison of your own making, eating nothing but preserved Iced VoVos and crystalline ginger. Honey everywhere. Pissing all the time (they say the altitude does that).

How does she get out of here? Alive?

Sunken rock

— *Don't go out in the sun for too long.*
— *Stick together; go with someone.*

Become a lizard. This is the only way to survive in this place. Lie in wait in the shade of a tree-cactus or a yucca. Sit it out in the radiant heat waiting for the night-blooming flowering of these plants to give you food and sustenance and sweet smell when it's cooler and your imagination can take shape — these cactuses and agaves that start budding on the south-eastern exposure of stem tips, away from the hotter west. That secrete nectar into their leaves and tubes, await pollination. That rely on the yucca moth to do the work of cross-fertilisation.

Under construction (railroads)

You are writing this sitting at the window of La Posada Hotel, Spanish for 'resting place', built by the acclaimed architect Mary Colter, in room number two hundred, the Carole Lombard room, overlooking the BNSF Railway (Burlington Northern Santa Fe Railway) and Amtrak station, one of the great American railroad stations in the City of Winslow on 303 East Second Street (Route 66), Arizona. It's a beautiful autumn day before the cool change, which is coming — predicted to bring snow farther up the line in Flagstaff and on the San Francisco Peaks. Your windows are open to the sun and the breeze, to the sounds of the track and the smell of diesel — if you miss one train, another is not far away down the line. There are some trains as long as ten thousand feet, according to the police who told you off earlier. That's three kilometres, and some need two or three engines in the middle and the end to push them along. Carriage after carriage after carriage after carriage.

Lookout

But just as suddenly the noise on the train line dies down in this place, it stops, and all you can hear is the sound of the wind through trees, cars on a distant highway going somewhere, and the laughter of small children in the garden just around the corner, singing some sort of future for themselves.

FRS: There is something about being in a faraway place, thirteen and a half thousand kilometres from home, that allows you to write about love, longing, desire — and regret. This ocean distance gives you permission to bring experiences of the heart up close, to see them strange, to write in the presence of the body. When I began this piece of nonfiction, '1:25,000', I didn't know what it was really about, what would turn up — the Grand Canyon, the pumpkin patch garden, the swing and the soft dirt, a sort of forgiveness of self: learning to say 'yes'. But there we are, all those words and sentences telling it slant, as Emily Dickinson would say: 'the truth must dazzle gradually / moderately'. '1:25,000' was born in Arizona, made of that place. The excuse to go to La Posada in Winslow was to have another WrICE experience. Let's call it WrICE Plus, David Carlin said. Let's do a residency à la WrICE after the nonfiction writing conference in Flagstaff — you know how it goes, all the writers stay at La Posada, we write all morning and meet together in the afternoon to read and share our work. La Posada is a vision of a hotel in the middle of the desert, a combination, someone says, of Mission Revival and Spanish Colonial Revival architecture styles. It'll be the best place to write,

David said. And so it was. The joy of present tense: the nowness of writing in the company of. And country: the convex shape of this land, saturated colour. There was an openness and vulnerability about this place.

AVIATION

Maxine Beneba Clarke

Mirabel plumps up the cushions and straightens the curtains. She walks nervously around the room to check everything's in place. She and Michael always talked about this day, about looking after kids of their own. And even though he isn't technically here with her, she *feels* him. All around.

It was golden outside like this, the day it all changed. That morning, on her walk, yellow light had flatlined uninterrupted off the teal-sapphire of San Francisco Bay. Mirabel was standing in the centre of the lounge room, where she's standing now. Her long auburn hair had been twisted up into a silver butterfly clip, several disobedient heat-limp strands clinging stubbornly to the back of her neck. Mirabel closes her eyes for a moment, recalling the blissful unthinkingness of that last calm half-hour, before she *knew*.

Mirabel stops fidgeting. She sits down, drawing her long legs up underneath her on the couch. The clock's almost gone ten. They'll soon be here. It was nearly fall, the day Michael was killed. But it still smelt like summer, like this. The breeze had drifted in the open windows, all cut grass, and neighbours barbecuing, and freshly laid bitumen from two streets down the block. The house had been almost completely packed up into large brown boxes for the move. Mirabel'd been marvelling at the emptiness of it. The crisp, clean walls and ample floor space had suddenly made her fall in love with the place again — brought back the potential she'd seen three years back, when she and Michael first moved in.

Before he took the new job, and proposed.

Before she'd agreed to move states with him.

Just as she was musing on the emptiness, there'd been that knock on the door: *rappata rappata rappata*. A frantic urgency.

Antonio double-checks the silver house number on the front door, knocks loudly. 'Here's your new home for the while, fingers crossed, little man.' He gently rests his hand on the top of Sunni's head.

The boy's baseball cap is pulled tightly over his head. His arms hang straight and stiff by his sides, as if he's trying to squeeze himself smaller. The straps of his small purple backpack dig in against his chubby shoulders.

Antonio wants to reach down and give the kid a hug, but he doesn't want to unsettle him. They can hear footsteps now, moving towards them from inside the house. Antonio takes a deep breath in.

This is the kind of moment he talked about last month when his Daddy and Mama came visiting. His Mama'd started on him as soon as he opened the door, shaking her head and click-clicking that tongue of hers as she wandered disapprovingly around his tiny apartment.

'Lord have mercy on my soul,' she said. 'You a half-black, half–Puerto Rican man who graduated top of the class from UCLA. And this is how you gonna spend that education, ayah? Running after these *troubled* kids?'

Close behind her'd been his Daddy: six-and-a-half silent foot of brown building-site muscle, wrapping himself around Antonio's tall slim frame. Smiling at him softly like: *That mama of yours is gonna calm down eventually, don't worry, I got you son.*

Standing on the doorstep with Sunni, Antonio prays for that kind of love to open the heavy pine door.

Mirabel readjusts the silver heart necklace on top of her cotton shirt as she walks slowly down the hallway towards the front door. Through the frosted double-glass, she can see a tall, lean silhouette next to a shorter one. Her stomach flips.

She stops walking, puts her hand on the wall to keep herself steady. She's on the plane again. Right inside the nose of the beast, looking through the cabin door and out through the cockpit. The plane is suspended in time, hovering wasp-like.

She's close enough to the first Trade Tower to see through the glass, across one entire floor. She can see thin French-manicured secretarial fingers, flying across a laptop keyboard.

A lean blonde-haired man is scribbling notes on a whiteboard, his back facing her, in one of the glass-walled meeting rooms.

He turns mid-sentence, and she can see it's her Michael. He stares back at her, through the window, disbelief on his face. Too paralysed to even run.

Mirabel fights against it — blinks the vision back. It's been almost three years now. She needs to be okay, to move on. She's talked through the fostering thing — with her counsellor, with her pastor. With her parents. Even with Michael's parents. She can do this.

'Ms Mirabel Adams?'

'Yes.'

The woman's dressed in cream slacks and a white cotton blouse, her hair twisted back into a loose plait. Antonio's surprised. Usually the emergency carers are older — grandmotherly types. Her cheeks are flushed pink, as though she's been running.

'Hi, I'm Antonio. We spoke earlier on the phone. And this,' he puts a gentle hand on the boy's back, nudges him forward, 'is Sunni.'

The woman looks down suddenly, almost as if she's shocked to see a child standing there.

'Oh yes, of course. Hello *Sunny*! I'm so glad you're here! Come in.'

They walk down the polished wooden floorboards of the hallway, into the impeccably tidy lounge. Antonio sits Sunni down next to him, on the peach-coloured leather couch. He can feel the little boy's body, already shaking as he looks around him.

Mirabel moves into the kitchen, fixes two cups of tea and an orange juice. The kid. She hasn't even spoken to the kid properly yet. Hasn't even looked at him straight. She doesn't want to be too pushy with him in these first few minutes. She puts the drinks onto a flowered serving tray with a plate of Oreos, walks carefully back to the lounge, and sets it on the coffee table.

'Sunny,' she says. 'I'm so glad to have you here. I have a room all ready for you. We can go and have a look now, if you like? How are you?'

Mirabel looks at him: his chubby tan arms, big brown eyes, furrowed black eyebrows, the oversized cap pulled firmly over his head. She quickly takes her eyes off the boy, and looks over at the man from the foster-care office. He stares back at her steadily.

'Sunni, you should probably take off your hat indoors,' the man says, not moving his eyes from her face.

The kid's bottom lip is trembling. He raises his hand to the front of the navy baseball cap, slowly removes it, and settles it into his lap. His cheeks are plump, rosier than Mirabel's ever seen a seven-year-old's. Wound tightly over his head is a piece of black, stretchy material. It conceals the boy's hair, and twists around to form a kind of material-covered bun. Mirabel suddenly feels sick.

*

'Are you alright, Ms Adams?'

Antonio moves over to where the woman's squatting, crouched next to the coffee table, in front of Sunni. Her face is drained white.

He reaches over and hands Sunni the glass of orange juice, helps the woman up, and escorts her into her kitchen. He pulls out an upholstered wooden dining chair, folds up a clean tea towel, wets it with cold water, and hands it to her.

'I wasn't expecting —' she says, dabbing at her face. 'I'm so sorry. I probably upset him. He looked scared ...'

'He is scared, Ms Adams,' says Antonio. 'I thought — we had you down for emergency care. For any child,' he reminds her pointedly. 'Did Jillian at the office not explain ... ?'

'Yes ... *any child*. I did say that,' Ms Adams says, shaking her head. 'But I never considered ... Jillian said his name was Sunny, and I just thought —'

'It is.' Antonio lowers his voice. 'His name is Sundeep. His family calls him Sunni, for short. He's a good kid. I mean, he really is. I don't think he'll be any trouble at all. It's *emergency care*, Ms Adams. Just for the weekend. Then we'll find somewhere a bit more permanent.'

Mirabel takes a deep breath, swallows past the lump that's formed in her throat. 'Is he ... ? I mean ...'

The man stares back at her, annoyance written in his sigh. 'His family's Sikh,' he says quietly. 'If that matters to you.'

Mirabel closes her eyes for a moment. She doesn't even

know what that word means, doesn't know what she's supposed to do here.

She looks through the kitchen door to where the chubby little boy is sitting with his shoulders curved over and his backpack still on.

It is golden outside. It still smells like summer, even though it's just gone fall.

The breeze drifting in the open windows is all cut grass, and neighbours barbecuing, and freshly laid bitumen.

The boy is looking at her now, with those sad, dark eyes.

MBC: The experience of attending the inaugural WrICE residency in January 2014 was one of the most memorable of my writing career. Being able to workshop with older, more experienced writers in a safe, culturally diverse space was a rare and treasured freedom. The mix of emerging, early career, and established authors made the group seem like a family of writers. My story, 'Aviation', is about three people from very different backgrounds thrown together to hopefully 'make' something good. Though a self-contained piece, it is also very much a beginning for all three characters, just as that first residency was for WrICE. Then too, 'Aviation' is about cultural assumptions, misunderstandings, and expectations. Antonio's mother feels that because he is of mixed Puerto Rican and African-American heritage, and has a top education, he should have chosen a different career path. Mirabel says she will foster any child in need but when a child arrives from a different ethno-religious background to what she expected, she suddenly becomes reluctant. Sunni is full of fear at yet another possible rejection on the basis of his ethnic background, but is unaware of the personal circumstances of Mirabel, which are contributing to her apprehension. Expectations, misunderstandings, and assumptions around writing, race, and culture: these are some of the issues we discussed during the residency, musing long into the night as the lights went down over Penang, in the downstairs common room of the Ren I Tang hotel.

WE GOT USED TO HERE FAST

Jennifer Down

In the morning we walk all the way to the beach to count puffer fish. Me five, her four, plus a dead rat. Lally crouches and pokes it with a stick. There are maggots squirming in there and it makes me feel crook. It's the second day of school holidays. It's not raining, but it's so cold the air feels wet. Lally picks up twigs and holds them like cigarettes. Her breath comes out in clouds. I can tell she's trying to be grown-up but she looks constipated. We walk all morning, up and down the creek, then to the train station, because that's the safe place to cross the freeway. By the time we get to the Snakepit, the footy's started. Lally's tired, which is sort of Mum's fault since she's the reason we had to stay out of the house. At half-time we find the sausage sizzle. The guy's wearing a Karingal guernsey but he's nice. He asks if we want a sausage each, and when I tell him I've only got sixty cents he gives us two anyway.

The spare key's been moved from under the mat at home.

Lally whispers *Knock, Sam*, and I say *Fuck off will you Lally*. We go around the back and I try to do the security door quietly. But inside the washing machine's banging against the wall, and there's a smell I can't work out. I realise I never checked if there was a weird car out the front. I get the maggoty feeling in my guts. It's like Lally knows. I feel her starfish hand grab a fistful of my T-shirt. We move towards the kitchen like we're chained together.

I don't recognise Nan at first. It's been a long time since I've seen her. She's wearing shorts. Her legs are like two brown sticks, speckled and skinny.

I thought you two had run away, she says, and holds out her arms for a hug. I want to ask what she's doing here but I don't in case that's rude. Lally's eyes are moving from me to Nan. Finally she asks: *Where's Mum?*

She's in bed. I thought we'd have some lunch, then we'll go and get some shopping done. Then we're going to pack. You two are coming with me for a bit. Come up and visit Granddad.

Do we have to go? Lally asks.

Yes, Nan says. *But it's gunna be a good time. We'll make an adventure.*

In the morning she wakes us so early the birds aren't even up. Lally's dead weight. Nan has to tug her arms into her windcheater, shove her feet into her sneakers. There's all dust and hair and grot in the velcro straps and it makes my tummy swim. We kiss Mum goodbye. She's even sleepier than Lal, but she stands in the doorway to wave us off, pulling her dressing-gown cord tight. Her teeth are chattering so loud I can hear them.

In the car Lally falls asleep again straight away, mouth open. Puffer fish. Once in a while a snore catches in her throat, and Nan and I do little smiles at each other. Then I fall asleep, too. When I wake up there's a bit of dribble crusted at the corner of my mouth and I hope Nan hasn't seen. It's just getting day. There are light streaks in the sky. The clock says 6.46. We pull into a McDonald's. Lally wakes up when the car stops, says *Where are we*. Nan says *I'll show you*. Inside we get a whole serve of pancakes each. I finish Lally's and then we pretend the empty white containers are UFOs. Nan spreads out a map on the table.

We'll see how we go today, she says. *Maybe we'll get to Dubbo. Maybe Coonabarabran*. We're going all the way to Toowoomba. Her fingernails are the colour of clam shells.

Where are we now?

Shepparton. See, near the border of New South Wales.

We've never been out of Victoria. I can tell Lally doesn't get it. There are lots of things I know and she doesn't, since I'm four years older.

The car trip takes forever. I move to the back seat. Me and Lally play that game where you make up a story by each saying a word at a time.

Once.

There.

Was.

A.

Ugly.

Very.

Lally, that doesn't make sense.

It does if you say little *next. Once there was a ugly, very little …*

She starts cackling again.

You'll lay an egg, Nan says.

When the stories get too rude, we lower our voices until we're whispering, and then we're not even joining our words to make a story anymore, just saying the worst ones we can think of. *Pissbuggerbumshitdickarseweebastardfuck.* I know a worse word, but I don't say it. That's another thing Lally doesn't know.

We drive all day. I've never been in a car that long. I reckon even Nan's got the wriggles, because she starts saying *Not much longer.* I sleep. When I wake up we're pulling into a car park in front of a giant satellite dish. Lally's sitting with her face pressed to the window.

What is it? she asks. *Sam? Is that a spaceship?*

It's a satellite, I say, even though I've never seen one that huge so I might be wrong.

It's a radio telescope, Nan says. *When they first walked on the moon, we all watched it on telly. And this station was the one with the signal that went out to the whole world. Even America.*

The place is empty. There's a visitors' centre with a café, plastic chairs, and striped umbrellas, but it's all packed up for the day. Out the front are two smaller satellite dishes, both white, facing each other. They're far apart, maybe the length of the school oval.

If you go and stand in front of one, Sam, Nan says, *and Lally, you stand in front of the other, and you whisper into the middle of the dish, you'll be able to hear each other.*

I don't believe her, and I can tell Lally doesn't, either. Nan just smiles. *True,* she says. *Gotta whisper, though.*

Lally looks from me to Nan, then trots off. I head for the other dish, feeling dumb. I lean in close.

Hi, Sam, I hear her say.

Hi, I whisper back.

I can hear you, she says. It sounds like she's right in my ear. I turn around to look. She's standing in her purple tracksuit facing the other dish. Her hands are cupped like she's telling it a secret.

Can you hear me, Sam?

Yes.

Do you think Mum's sad because we left her?

No, Lal.

When do you think we'll go home?

I don't know.

Do you think she knows where we are?

I don't know.

Do you think she misses us?

Yes.

I glance over my shoulder. Nan's waiting with her arms crossed, but in a nice way, like we've got time.

We keep driving to Dubbo. It's dark when we get there. We've been in the car the whole day. I ask if we're gunna sleep in the car and Nan says no. We drive around some more looking for a motel. There's no room at the first two. *Like the story of the baby Jesus*, Lally says, and Nan laughs. *You'll lay an egg*, Lally dares, and I tell her not to be cheeky but Nan just keeps laughing until she's wheezing. We find a motel. There's a paper strip across the toilet seat. I crack Lally up by pretending it's a present wrapped up for me. We go for tea at a Chinese restaurant with thick red carpet. Walking back to the motel we stop at a payphone so Nan can call Granddad. Lally's pretending to smoke again, cloudy breath. I'm hopping from foot to foot. Nan doesn't seem to feel the cold at all. The orange phone booth light hangs over her.

In the dark later, Lally says my name. *Do you think we could make them dishes?* she asks. For a second I think she's talking about the beef and black bean we had for tea.

What are you talking about, you whacker?

The whispering satellites.

Go to sleep, Lal, chrissake.

If we could make that in our house, she says, *we could talk without Mum being angry.*

*

The day he was discharged, we waited all morning for the specialist to come in, then the surgeon, then we waited for the paperwork. No one seemed to know what was going on. Lunch.

He was supposed to be gone by then. I had to argue until he got a meal. He had a spoonful of mashed potato and pushed the rest away. A shift change. I waited by the nurses' station, ready for a fight. He stood beside me. He leaned against the wall. His face was pinched and grey.

I was so full of rage that I didn't notice him fading. When I turned he was sitting in a plastic chair by the elevator, barely upright. His earlobes poked out from his woollen hat.

Outside he ripped the plastic band from his wrist. He wanted to go to his ex-boyfriend's house. They'd been separated for six months by then, but they were still close. He phoned a cab. I tried to go with him.

'I'll go home and get my car, and drop you round,' I said. 'Theo'd hate to see you pull up in a taxi by yourself. Just wait here half an hour.'

'I've fucken waited all morning.'

'Will you please do this one thing for me.'

'I just want to go,' he said.

The taxi arrived. I put his bag on the seat beside him, tugged his beanie down to cover his ears.

At home I moved from room to room. It was as quiet as a church. When I think of him now it's getting into the car by himself, crabbed like a frightened child. He weighed fifty-eight kilos.

*

When it's Easter I'm twelve and Lally's eight, and we've been in Toowoomba for almost a year. Lally peed the bed every night for three weeks, but Nan never got angry once. I think I'm meant to remember Mum's face but it's sort of swirly in my head. We got used to here fast. We got used to Granddad, his menthols and his radio and his pill pack that the pharmacy girl drops in every week. His funny sayings like *colder than a frog's fart*. He teases Nan about believing in baby Jesus until Lally declares she believes in baby Jesus, too. He took us to the pet shop in town and bought us a guinea pig. We did a vote and named him Harry. Granddad loves shows and stories about mysteries, but not the sort police detectives can solve. His favourite mystery is about two guys who died on a hill in a jungle in Brazil. No one knew how they died but they were found wearing raincoats and eye masks, like ones rich ladies wear to bed in the movies, only made out of lead. One of them also had a note that read: *16:30 be at the determined place. 18:30 swallow capsules, after effect protect metals wait for mask signal.* That's the part that really gets Granddad going.

It's April when the phone calls start again. Mum starts wanting to speak to me and Lally. It feels sad, like she's left out, so I try to make it sound like things are boring. It's sort of true, but I like it. The weeks have a regular heartbeat. Tuesdays we go to the RSL because it's eight-dollar seniors' meals, then Nan plays the pokies. Thursday's pension day, which is groceries then fish and chips. Friday's swimming practice.

Lally and I are playing Power Rangers in the backyard. It's her favourite game but I hardly ever play it with her because I'm embarrassed. Granddad says *Mum's on the phone* and we ignore him for a bit but then we go in. Straight away Mum's voice sounds different, like she's swallowed some colour. She asks heaps of questions. It reminds me of when she was in love with Gary and she laughed all the time. She says *How about if I come up to visit.* Nan and Granddad are smiling at me and Lally's going *What, what Sam, what's she saying.* I don't know why, but my guts go bad. I talk for a bit longer, then I push the phone at Lally. I lock myself in the old outdoor toilet. Bad watery shit comes out of me and I know it's because I'm guilty and I don't want Mum to come.

After tea Nan and Granddad tell us we can play in the backyard a bit longer, but Lally and me squat on the bricks under the kitchen window so we can hear them talking inside. It smells like rain even though a storm hasn't come yet. Nan and Granddad are talking back and forth, but not in a way of arguing. They keep saying *She* and I can't work out if they mean Mum or Lally or someone else. They keep saying *Custardy.* The crickets are so loud it's hard to hear much else.

What's custardy, I say, even though it's not like Lally's gunna know. But she puts a finger to her lips.

It's who owns the kids, she whispers.

How do you know that?

She shrugs. It pisses me off, the way she knows something I don't, the bored way she explains it. I'm suddenly so mad that my body can't hold it in. I reach out and shove Lally hard. She flies backwards and lands on her bum on the bricks. Her head hits the corner of the card table. She scrunches her eyes closed. I wait for her to cry, but she doesn't make a noise. The floodlight flicks on and Granddad's in the doorway. He says *Come on, it's dark. Jump in the bath, Lal,* and she trails inside after him. Doesn't look back.

*

He was back in the hospital four days later, worse than before. He had two transfusions in a week. I called Theo, who came straight away. He sat on the end of the bed.

'When I didn't hear from you after the other night,' he said, 'I got worried you'd gone off to die by yourself like a dog.'

They had a fight right there in the room. I kept trying to leave but they both wanted me to witness it. We all cried. Theo left.

Sam asked what the weather was like outside. I told him it was pissing down.

'Remember when we got stuck in that motel room in Coffs Harbour during the floods?' I said.

'Mm,' he said.

'And then bananas got really expensive,' I said.

'All the sugarcane was fucked.'

'That was coming down, with Mum,' I said. 'Remember on the drive up with Nan when we stayed at the Peter Allen motel in Tenterfield?'

'She had the tape of him. She played it in the car.'

'Remember when she came to get us? She was wearing that jacket. Hot pink, made out of, like, parachute material.'

'I just remember her shorts. Middle of winter.'

'We stopped at the whispering dishes at that CSIRO place,' I said.

'I don't want to speak about it anymore,' he said.

He thinks I never forgave him for what happened but it's not true. I know he couldn't have helped it. I hated being split up, but that's what happens to 'sibling groups'. That's what we were called. No one takes you in twos. Nan and Granddad would have, but by then Nan was wandering at dusk and forgetting to eat, and Granddad couldn't look after three of us.

Sam was at the age where they try to *transition* you out of resi and into independent living. They put him up in a motel room. I got to visit him once. The caseworker left us alone, at least. Sam made us instant coffee with powdered milk. It made my heart go too fast. He'd stopped going to school by then. He said he felt like he was in jail. He asked me how I was going. I was feeling mean, so I told him about how a boy tried to fuck me with a beer bottle. He got so angry I thought he was going to tear a hole in the world. That was not long before he got sick the first time. I've never seen him look as mighty since.

*

Lally and I walk home from school trying to solve the mystery of the lead mask men. Lally reckons the masks were like sleeping masks, only magic, and instead of putting the men to sleep, they sent their souls somewhere else, like heaven maybe, only their bodies got left behind. We're crossing under the rail bridge, almost at the big park on O'Quinn Street, ready to cut across the grass when I feel a tap on my shoulder. Tegan Foster's standing there with her little sister, who's younger than Lally.

She says *Hey* and I say *Hey* back even though I just saw her at school. Her bag hook's near mine.

She says *What are you guys talking about* and Lally starts telling her the whole story. Sometimes I have to interrupt because she leaves out important bits. I feel dumb, though, and when Tegan looks at me it feels like my face is shrinking. She's standing with her hand on her hip. I wait for her to laugh, but she just says *Maybe they were time travellers, and the pills sent them* — she waves her hand. The four of us stand there. Tegan's sister says *Are we going?* and Tegan says *You guys go and play on the playground* and we all know she means the little girls. Lally looks dubiously at the patch of tanbark, but they take off running, schoolbags jumping up and down on their shoulders.

Tegan says *C'mere* and starts walking back towards school, towards the low rail bridge. I'm following her brown ponytail, blue scrunchie, past the beams painted red and white stripes, past the sign that says LOW CLEARANCE 2.6m, through the broken bit of the wire fence, up the muddy rise, over the stones and pieces of glass and dirt until we're right underneath the train tracks. We both have to crouch. I can feel the sweat pricking the behinds of my knees. Then she kisses me. It's sort of a surprise but sort of not. Her mouth is warm and I hope I'm doing it right. I keep my eyes closed so I can concentrate. She says *Open your teeth, dummy*, and I unclench my mouth a bit, and her tongue goes in. I'm holding both Tegan's hands. I don't remember grabbing them. It feels like an earthquake's coming, but then I realise it's only a train going over us. We stop kissing to listen. This close, it sounds like the end of the world.

Suddenly Lally's standing down below, near the hole in the fence. *That playground's shit*, she says. Tegan laughs and lets go my hands. She says *Where's Jadie*. We crab-crawl down the slope and walk back towards the park. Tegan's sister is waiting by the dunny block with its painted mural. After that Tegan and I hold hands sometimes at school when we line up for assembly. Some days we go to sit in the concrete pipes to kiss. Lally knows she's not invited.

We have a working bee to get ready for Mum. Granddad shows me how to mow the lawn. We're out the front doing the edges when Nan starts yelling. We both run, but I'm fastest, and when I get to the backyard I see her holding Lally by the shoulders and she's screaming *What were you doing, what were you doing*. She's shaking Lally so hard that Lal's head is bobbing on the stalk of her neck. I look to see if Lally's peed but she hasn't. Nan's the one who's upset; Lal just looks bored. Then Granddad's there and he says *Stop, Shirl. What happened?* And that's when I see Harry the guinea pig in the fresh-cut grass by Lally's feet, and I know he's dead. Nan lets go Lally's shoulders. *She had it like this* — she's speaking to Granddad, holding her hands like there's a sandwich in them — *and she squeezed it 'til it died. She looked right at me.* Her voice is high and rattly. Lally bursts into tears. They're terrible sobs that come up out of her legs. *All right*, Granddad says. *I'm sure it was an accident. It's all right.* In that second I see Nan decide it was an accident, too. She takes Lally into her arms. Later

Granddad and I put Harry in a tissue box and bury him under the hibiscus.

School breaks up on Friday. On Saturday Mum arrives and says she's taking us back to Melbourne.

*

That last night I came straight from work. Theo had already left. It was dark out.

'The oncologist was supposed to come again at eight,' Sam said, 'but I don't think he's coming now.'

'I don't think he's coming, either,' I said. I went to stand by the window. Outside, below, the suburbs were pricked with light.

'I'm scared,' he said.

'I'm going to stay with you all night,' I said. 'I just want to nick downstairs and get a Coke. Okay?'

When I got back he'd torn out the drip, the one they'd had so much trouble getting in because his veins had collapsed. It seemed like there was a lot of blood.

'The fuck are you doing?'

'Help me, Lal,' he said. His eyes were real dry. 'I don't want to stay here.'

'You're going to get an infection.'

'I'll get one anyway.'

He listed in the bed, pressing a cotton patch to the crook of his arm where the shunt had been. I remembered after the bone marrow transplant the first time, ten years ago, when he got pneumonia and almost drowned in his own lung-shit.

'Where do you wanna go?' I asked.

'Country,' he said. 'Out where the dish is. Do you remember that? When Nan took us?'

'Of course I do. But that's hours away. That's up near Forbes.'

'If you don't want to,' he said, 'I will take myself.'

'What about Theo?'

'I just want you to take me,' he said. 'I'm sorry. I'm sorry.'

'It's all right.'

I dressed him in clean clothes. I brought the car around, parked it in a five-minute zone while I went upstairs to sneak him out. I felt frightened, and he could tell. It was the first time I'd seen him smile in days.

'We're not robbing a bank,' he said.

'You're supposed to *tell* them when you leave,' I hissed. If he could have laughed, he would have.

We drove all night. At first I talked to him to keep him awake. I was scared he'd drop off and slip away for good. But sleep dragged him down. I arranged my coat around him to cushion his body, leaned his car seat back. I could smell us both: my sweat and his chemicals.

'You gunna crash?' he croaked once.

'What? No,' I said, humourless, not understanding.

'Then can you take off my seatbelt? It's giving me the shits.'

The moon slipped away. I sang to myself to stay awake.

I bought coffee and lollies at the servo. I had to help him sit on the toilet. He was too weak to stand up to piss.

Close to dawn I pulled into a truck stop.

'We're nearly there but I have to sleep,' I said. 'I'm knackered.'

I pushed my seat back, made myself a nest of jumpers and blankets.

'Tell me the story of the lead masks,' he said.

'I'll tell you when we get to the dish.' The sky was silver, the long grass very still. The roos were crouched by the highway.

He was shaking then and I knew I should have taken him to the closest base hospital, but I've always been glad I didn't.

JD: Movement always makes my brain work better. It doesn't have to be anywhere exotic: a train ride will help. But I'm also fascinated by our personal geographies — the way memories are pinned to certain sites. In Penang I got up every morning and walked down Lebuh King towards the esplanade by the sea. There was a park with dry grass where groups of men played cricket and did tai chi. A small basketball court, silent in the pink, hazy dawn. There was a thickness to the air. The leaves overhead did not move. A group of elderly people walked brisk circles around the concrete edging the park. I walked to the seawall and sat with my legs dangling over the edge. I walked back to the hotel past the ferry terminal, stopping for coffee and roti canai. There is a greasy smudge in the Leslie Marmon Silko book I was reading at the time. The rest of our days were ordered, too: we kept to ourselves of a morning, and came together to workshop in the afternoons. It's strange to make a routine like that knowing you can keep it only for a week, to fashion order and familiarity from transience. When I wrote the story in this collection, it had been two years since my residency, where I got to talk and workshop and swap recommendations with writers whose work I much admired. I wrote it thinking about transience and boundaries and memory. How we try to give meaning to terrible things; how we try to make order of chaos; how much we can ask of others.

NOTES ON WrICE

From the founders

WrICE grew from earlier projects Francesca and I had run out of RMIT's creative-writing programs and our non/fictionLab research group in Melbourne, which were all about curating new environments for creative collaboration: for instance, artist-in-residence programs bringing Australian writers and artists such as Hannie Rayson, Christos Tsiolkas, Kim Scott, and Mandy Ord in contact with our students, and mini collaborative residencies and workshops mixing faculty and student writers with visiting international authors such as Robin Hemley and Patricia Foster. Contact with writers from the region through Asia Pacific Writers and Translators conferences opened our eyes to the obvious: Australia's literary culture was much the poorer through being cut off from the wealth of cultural traditions evolving, and the myriad conversations happening, just to the north. There are already excellent and long-established individual residency programs available to Australians, so we wanted to do something different — build cultural understanding by bringing writers together, across a table, away somewhere. And we asked ourselves: well, what would *we* like? — *David Carlin*

Remember, the dream came first: imagine if? Then we followed our instinct, delighting in going back and forth to tease out possibilities, before alighting on a single word, both acronym and homophone, to capture what it was we were aiming for: WrICE. Writers Immersion and Cultural Exchange. It was to be all about writers and writing, to give us sustenance, an exchange for writers practising in this region — we wanted it to go across borders and nationalities, to intersect different cultures; something a group of writers could do together to draw our countries closer in friendship and conviviality. And immersion: we wanted it to be a face-to-face exchange, an immersive experience and a collaborative workshop for writers, without a hierarchy separating the more-experienced writers from those emerging. What we are proudest of is the presence of the emerging writers, students and graduates of our RMIT programs, who have gone on after WrICE to publish in their own right: to take their place confidently as professional writers. It was an audacious idea — creating space for a joint residency to bring writers together who didn't necessarily know one another. Now: who would join us? — *Francesca Rendle-Short*

From alumni

The fostering of a strong Asia-Pacific writing community, and the exchange of ideas and experiences within that community, is vital to the growth and survival of Australian literature, and of particular importance to me, as a first-generation Australian writer of colour. It's given me new and exciting ideas about genre, practice, and form borne out of intense roundtable discussions and the vast collective experience of participants in the WrICE program. It's given me a magical space away from the time constraints and the social and familial obligations of everyday life.　　　　　　　　 — *Maxine Beneba Clarke*

I think it's imperative that we as Australian artists engage with the cultures of South-East Asia, as Australia is part of the region but often uneasy about its neighbours. As a person whose heritage straddles both South-East Asia and Australia, much of my work has dealt with this push-and-pull. I see this as a unique opportunity to explore a rich culture that is rapidly modernising, but has ancient roots, through poetry, music, and art.　　　　　　　　　　　　　 — *Omar Musa*

Asia-Pacific communities need to find our own sustainable ways of speaking among ourselves and relating to one another as cultural practitioners with mutual respect and a sense of vibrant possibility. Our young writers need to grow up *with* one another instead of merely side-by-side. As an alternative and promising prototype for quickly building connections between writers across borders, the WrICE model — regularly and judiciously proliferated across the region — could transform the region's literary and cultural perspectives.   — *Alvin Pang*

I knew so little about Vietnam — in fact, I didn't even know Hanoi had four seasons; I just assumed it was like the Philippines because of its geographical proximity. It was my first experience of winter, and I was completely unprepared! But aside from our historical connections, I saw how different we truly were as Asians. The cultural exchange intensified my sense of how my writing can (and should) be a way to assert my Philippine identity.   — *Jhoanna Lynn B. Cruz*

As an Aboriginal writer I have long been interested in Australia's role as a creative powerhouse within the Asia-Pacific. Yet engagement with Asian and Pacific writers has usually eluded me, except fleetingly at festivals. I was interested to sit for a week and really dig down with writers from other nearby cultures (what we in Aboriginal English call 'Proper Neighbour Country') into what they are attempting in their works. How do they see Australia, and Aboriginal people in particular? I'd also like to respectfully offer a twenty-first-century Aboriginal perspective on their creative work and on the cultural paradigms they bring to the table.   — *Melissa Lucashenko*

For more information and to follow the ongoing story, visit
www.wrice.com.au

CONTRIBUTORS

David Carlin is an award-winning writer and creative artist. His books include *The Abyssinian Contortionist*, *Our Father Who Wasn't There*, and *Performing Digital*. David wrote and co-produced the radiophonic feature *Making Up*, which won four Gold and Silver awards at the 2016 New York Festivals International Radio Awards. David is vice-president of the international NonfictioNOW Conference, and Associate Professor of Creative Writing, co-founder of the non/fictionLab research group, and co-director of the WrICE program at RMIT University.

Bernice Chauly is the author of five books of poetry and prose, including the award-winning memoir *Growing Up with Ghosts*. She lectures in creative writing at the University of Nottingham Malaysia Campus and is the Director of the George Town Literary Festival. She is currently editing her first novel, which begins during the Malaysian Reformasi movement of 1998.

Maxine Beneba Clarke is an Australian writer of Afro-Caribbean heritage. She is the author of the poetry collection *Carrying the World*. Maxine's first collection of short fiction won the 2013

Victorian Premier's Literary Award for an Unpublished Manuscript, the 2015 ABIA Award for Best Literary Fiction, and the 2015 Indie Award for debut fiction, and saw her named a *Sydney Morning Herald* Best Young Australian Novelist. Her memoir, *The Hate Race*, and her children's picture book, *The Patchwork Bike*, were published in 2016.

Jhoanna Lynn B. Cruz is an award-winning writer who teaches literature and creative writing at the University of the Philippines Mindanao. Her first book, *Women Loving: stories and a play* (2010), is the first sole-author anthology of lesbian-themed stories in the Philippines. Cruz is president of the Davao Writers Guild and is Regional Coordinator for Southern Mindanao in the National Committee on Literary Arts. Her stories are available as an eBook entitled *Women on Fire*, and her nonfiction has recently appeared in *Griffith Review*.

Jennifer Down is a writer, editor, and translator. Her work has appeared in *The Saturday Paper*, *Australian Book Review*, *Overland*, *Kill Your Darlings*, and *The Lifted Brow*. Her novel *Our Magic Hour* is available through Text Publishing.

Laurel Fantauzzo grew up in California with a Filipina mother and an Italian-American father. Her work has appeared in the *New York Times*, *Esquire Philippines*, and *The Rumpus*, among other venues, and she recently earned grants and residencies from Erasmus and Hedgebrook. She is an instructor and an emerging-writer-in-residence at Yale-NUS.

Amarlie Foster lives in Melbourne. Her writing has appeared in *Cordite Poetry Review* and *Rabbit*. In 2015 she was shortlisted for the *Overland* Victoria University Short Story Prize for New and Emerging Writers.

Robin Hemley has published twelve books and has won numerous literary awards, including a Guggenheim Fellowship, three Pushcart Prizes, the Independent Press Book Award, and fellowships from the Bogliasco Foundation and the MacDowell Colony. His work has been published in the United States, Britain, Canada, Australia, Japan, Germany, the Philippines, and elsewhere. A graduate of the Iowa Writers Workshop, he returned to Iowa to direct the Nonfiction Writing Program before moving to Yale-NUS College in Singapore to direct the writing program and serve as writer-in-residence. He is Adjunct (Distinguished) Professor in Creative Writing at RMIT University.

Cate Kennedy is a novelist, short-story writer, poet, and essayist. Her most recent story collection, *Like a House on Fire*, won a Queensland Literary Award and was shortlisted for the inaugural Stella Prize and the Kibble Award. Her third poetry collection, *The Taste of River Water*, won a Victorian Premier's Literary Award, and her novel, *The World Beneath*, was shortlisted for the *Age* Book of the Year Award, the Barbara Jefferis Award, and the NSW Premier's Prize for Fiction. Cate is a fiction advisor at Pacific University, Oregon, in their MFA program.

Suchen Christine Lim is an award-winning Singaporean writer, and the author of five novels, a short-story collection, a play, and several children's books. The recipient of a Fulbright grant, she was International Writing Fellow and writer-in-residence at the University of Iowa, and a Visiting Fellow in Creative Writing at the Nanyang Technological University of Singapore, and in 2012 she received the Southeast Asia Write Award. Her novel *Fistful of Colours* won the inaugural Singapore Literature Prize, and her latest novel, *The River's Song*, was featured in *Kirkus Reviews'* 100 Best Books of 2015.

Melissa Lucashenko is an award-winning Aboriginal novelist who lives between Brisbane and the Bundjalung nation. Her writing explores the stories and passions of ordinary Australians with particular reference to Aboriginal people and those living on the margins of the First World. Melissa's most recent book, *Mullumbimby*, is a critically acclaimed novel of romantic love and cultural warfare set in a remote valley in the state of New South Wales, Australia.

Harriet McKnight was shortlisted for the 2014 *Overland* Victoria University Short Story Prize and the 2015 ABR Elizabeth Jolley Short Story Prize. Her work appears in *Australian Book Review* and *Westerly*. Since 2013 Harriet has been the deputy editor of *The Canary Press*. Her first novel will be published by Black Inc. in 2017.

Omar Musa is a Malaysian-Australian author, rapper, and poet from Queanbeyan, Australia. He is the former winner of the Australian

Poetry Slam and the Indian Ocean Poetry Slam. Omar has appeared on ABC's *Q&A* and received a standing ovation at TEDx Sydney at the Sydney Opera House. His debut novel, *Here Come the Dogs*, was longlisted for the Miles Franklin Award and the International Dublin Literary Award, and he was named one of the *Sydney Morning Herald*'s Best Young Australian Novelists in 2015.

Nguyen Bao Chan is a Vietnamese poet. Her works include *Burned River*, which won a Vietnamese Literary and Arts Union award; *Barefoot in Winter*, and *Thorns in Dreams*. She has performed at literary festivals around the world, including in Colombia (at the prestigious International Poetry Festival of Medellín), London, and France, and she currently works as an editor in the Vietnamese television industry.

Melody Paloma is a Melbourne-based poet. Her work has appeared in *Overland*, *Rabbit*, and *Voiceworks*, and she was awarded the 2014 *Overland* Judith Wright Poetry Prize for New and Emerging Poets. Melody is founder and editor of Dear Everybody (@deareverybodycollective), a creative collective facilitating collaboration and creative exchange between artists and writers.

Alvin Pang is an award-winning poet, writer, editor, anthologist, and translator. His works have been translated into more than fifteen languages and he has appeared at festivals and in publications worldwide. He is also editor-in-chief of *Ethos*, a Singaporean public policy journal, and directs The Literary Centre (Singapore), a non-profit intercultural platform.

Alice Pung is a Melbourne writer, journalist, and essayist. Her books *Unpolished Gem*, *Her Father's Daughter*, and *Laurinda* have all been shortlisted for or won major Australian writing awards, and her anthology, *Growing up Asian in Australia*, is a regular set text for high-school students. Alice is also a contributor to *The Monthly*, *The Age*, *Good Weekend*, and *The Australian*, and her work has appeared in the *Best Australian Stories* and *Best Australian Essays* series.

Francesca Rendle-Short is an award-winning novelist, memoirist, and essayist. She is the author of *Imago* and the acclaimed novel-cum-memoir *Bite Your Tongue*. Her work has appeared in a wide range of Australian and international publications, including *Best Australian Science Writing*, *Overland*, and *The Essay Review*, and her artwork is in the collection of the State Library of Queensland. Francesca is Associate Professor of Creative Writing at RMIT University, where she is co-founder and co-director of the non/fictionLab research group and the WrICE program.

Joe Rubbo is a Melbourne-based writer. He has recently completed an Associate Degree in Professional Writing and Editing at RMIT. He has worked, among other jobs, as a chef, a technical writer for a construction company, and an English teacher in Italy. He now works at a reputable Melbourne bookstore.

Laura Stortenbeker is a Melbourne-based writer and editor. In 2015 she placed second in the Josephine Ulrick Literature Prize. Her work has appeared in *Overland*, *Chart Collective*, and the *Review of Australian Fiction*.

Nyein Way is a poet, performance artist, and educator. He has published seven books of poetry, most recently *A Handbook for Paranothingness*, *A Post-Conceptual Dictionary*, and *Total Poetry*. He was a resident artist of Mekong Art Project in Cambodia, and has held workshops and readings in Cambodia, Thailand, the United States, and Myanmar. The chief cultural advisor for the New Yangon Theatre Institute, he has also appeared at the Queensland Poetry Festival.

Xu Xi is the author of ten books, including the novel *That Man in Our Lives;* the short-story collection *Access;* and the novel *Habit of a Foreign Sky*, a finalist for the Man Asian Literary Prize. Forthcoming books include *Interruptions*, a collaborative ekphrastic essay collection in conversation with photography by David Clarke; *Elegy for HK*, a memoir; and *Insignificance: stories of Hong Kong*, a collection of short fiction. A Chinese-Indonesian native of Hong Kong and a US citizen, she lives between New York and Hong Kong.

ACKNOWLEDGEMENTS

This book couldn't have come into being if it wasn't for all the writers whose work is represented in these pages. This book is because of you and about you and made in honour of what we've started together.

Thank you to Alice Pung for your beautiful foreword. We are so thrilled you are part of this book; doubly so because you are a WrICE Fellow for the China/Melbourne program in 2016.

Thank you to the inimitable Ronnie Scott for taking charge of the production editing and helping bring the book together with such panache, style, and energy. We are so grateful for your editing chops, diligence, international diplomacy, thoughtfulness, and sense of humour — oh, and lightning-fast email turnarounds.

Thank you to Julia Carlomagno and Henry Rosenbloom at Scribe Publications, for your openness to and appreciation of the vision for WrICE and for what this book could be.

Thank you to our colleagues and creators-in-arms in the non/fictionLab at RMIT University. The pleasure it is to be part of such an energetic and supportive bunch of people. In particular, to Tracy O'Shaughnessy, who helped broker the early stages of this publishing venture and then continued to give brilliant advice thereafter. Your enthusiasm for the project, wisdom, professionalism, and support was invaluable — and saw us through. To Ali Barker for making the practicalities of our WrICE project sing: we couldn't do it without you. To Clare Renner for joining us in WrICE as co-director: your presence in both Singapore and Vietnam was indispensable.

Thank you to the other supporters of this book and project at RMIT University, including Martyn Hook, Paul Gough, Tania Lewis, Jonathan Laskovsky, Jonathan O'Donnell, Melissa Smith, Saskia Hansen, Penny Johnson, and many more.

Thanks to our brilliant WrICE project partners in 2014 and 2015, including the Melbourne Writers Festival, the Emerging Writers' Festival, *Peril* magazine, Footscray Community Arts Centre, the Castlemaine literary community, The Wheeler Centre, Singapore Arts House, BooksActually in Singapore, Yale NUS College in Singapore, the National Library of Vietnam, Thế Giới Publishers, and Manzi Café in Hanoi. In particular, thanks to Lisa Dempster, Sam Twyford-Moore, Kate Callingham, Lian Low, Alia Gabres, Terence Jaensch, Maggie Fooke, Kenny Leck, Karen Choo, Lisa Marie Lip, and Tram Vu.

Finally, enormous thanks to the Copyright Agency Cultural Fund, and to Zoe Rodriguez and Jim Alexander, for taking the risk in supporting the WrICE project so generously and creatively from the beginning.

Versions of these pieces have previously appeared in the following places:

'Unmade in Bangkok' by David Carlin as part of a radiophonic essay feature called *Making Up: eleven scenes from a Bangkok hotel*, co-produced by Kyla Brettle and David Carlin for ABC Radio National's *Soundproof*, 2015.

'Standing in the Eyes of the World' by Bernice Chauly (as 'The New Gods'), in *Ducts*, issue 36, 2015.

'Comadrona' by Jhoanna Lynn B. Cruz in *Women Loving*, De La Salle University and Anvil Publishing, Inc., 2010, and in *Women on Fire*, Master Publishing/The Can-Do! Company, 2015.

'Some Hints About Travelling to the Country Your Family Departed' by Laurel Fantauzzo in *Leap Plus*, edited by Angelo R. Lacuesta, published in conjunction with the Asia Pacific Writers & Translators Conference held in Manila, Philippines, 2015.

'My Two Mothers' by Suchen Christine Lim in *The Lies That Build a Marriage*, Monsoon Books, 2007.

'Dreamers' by Melissa Lucashenko as a play commissioned by Northern Rivers Performing Arts, 2015.

'Terra Nullius' by Harriet McKnight in *The Suburban Review*, volume 6, 2015, and 'Rip Current' by Harriet McKnight in *The Suburban Review*, online, 2015.

'The Train of Time' by Nguyen Bao Chan as 'Chuyến tàu' in *Văn Nghệ Quân Đội*, 2014, and 'Missing' by Nguyen Bao Chan as 'Vắng' in *Nhân Dân*, 2013.

'The Illoi of Kantimeral' by Alvin Pang in the anthology *COAST*, edited by Lee Wei Fen and Daren Shiau, Math Paper Press, 2011, and in *Best New Singapore Short Stories*, volume 1, Epigram, 2013.

'Floodlit' by Laura Stortenbeker in *Review of Australian Fiction*, volume 14, issue 3, 2015.

'BG: the significant years' by Xu Xi in *Hotel Amerika*, Chicago, volume 8, number 2, 2010.

Some of the pieces in this collection contain material quoted from other sources.

The quote from Albert Einstein on page 144 of 'BG: the significant years' by Xu Xi is from Autograph Document, Draft, 28–844, reproduced with grateful acknowledgement to the Albert Einstein Archives at the Hebrew University of Jerusalem.

The quote from Vietnam Online on page 136 of 'Incoming Tides' by Cate Kennedy is reproduced with kind permission of Vietnam Online, http://www.vietnamonline.com/destination/hanoi.html.

The poem on page 222 is taken from '*The Gorgeous Nothings: Emily Dickinson's Envelope Poems*' by Emily Dickinson, edited by Jen Bervin and Marta Werner, New Directions, 2013.

Some of the dialogue in 'Unmade in Bangkok' by David Carlin is drawn from the following sources and is reproduced with kind permission of the publishers: *Gender Trouble: feminism and the subversion of identity* by Judith Butler, New York, Routledge, 1999; *Three Steps on the Ladder of Writing* by Hélène Cixous, trans. S. Cornell and S. Sellers, New York,

Columbia University Press, 1993, p.51; *Hotel Theory* by Wayne Koestenbaum, Berkeley, Soft Skull Press, 2007; 'Of Experience' by Michel de Montaigne, in *Essays*, Stanford University Press, 1958 (first published 1580); *A Room of One's Own* by Virginia Woolf, New York, Harcourt Brace & Co, 1989 (first published 1929); and *Orlando* by Virginia Woolf, London, Hogarth Press, 1928.